Bull Catcher

Alden R. Carter

SCHOLASTIC
Signature

an imprint of
Scholastic Inc.

New York · Toronto · London · Auckland · Sydney
Mexico City · New Delhi · Hong Kong

ACKNOWLEDGMENTS

Many thanks to all who helped with *Bull Catcher*, particularly my
editor, Anne Dunn; my mother, Hilda Carter Fletcher; my son, Brian
(a catcher); my daughter, Siri (also a catcher); and my friends Regina
Griffin, Don Gallo, Steve Sanders, and Dean Markwardt. I owe special thanks to my friend Graham Olson, who read and re-read the
manuscript from the standpoint of coach, teacher, and one-time
catcher. As always, my wife, Carol, deserves much of the credit.

12 11 10 9 8 7 6 5 4 3 2 1   0 1 2 3 4 5/0

Printed in the U.S.A.   01

First Scholastic Trade paperback printing, March 2000

Praise for
ALDEN R. CARTER'S
BULL CATCHER

"Unlike many sports novels, *Bull Catcher* does more than pump up its readers for a do-or-die game against the crosstown rivals. Carter takes a deeper look at sports, competition, and what it takes to succeed."

— *Booklist*

"[An] engaging novel. . . . And the author clearly knows the game, too. Its dynamics, as played on the high school level, are perfectly delineated. . . . Baseball fans will relish the exciting game descriptions and the evocation of a team maturing over a four-year span of big wins and tough losses. Baseball fans will certainly enjoy this."

— *VOYA*

"Carter pens a sure hit for baseball fans as plenty of riveting game action is detailed. This is a gentle coming-of-age story that results in an enjoyable read."

— *SLJ*

"The complex relationships between Bull and his family, girlfriends, and teammates are skillfully depicted."

— *Horn Book*

"Carter traces a boy's growth from baseball fanaticism to athletic wisdom in a gritty story of teenage love and loss."

— *The ALAN Review*

American Bookseller Pick of the Lists

An ALA Best Book for Young Adults

An ALA "Quick Pick"

Arthur Tofte Juvenile Fiction Book Award
(Council of Wisconsin Writers)

750L

OTHER SIGNATURE TITLES

Between a Rock and a Hard Place
Alden R. Carter

Dogwolf
Alden R. Carter

Slam!
Walter Dean Myers

Jonah, the Whale
Susan Shreve

Pirate's Son
Geraldine McCaughrean

Somewhere in the Darkness
Walter Dean Myers

Tangerine
Edward Bloor

For some friends:

*Graham Olson, Walt Chapman, Ron O'Brien,
and Duwayne and Sue Jacobson*

Bull Catcher

ME (AND JEFF)

Coming down the line between third and home, you'll find the Bull. That's me, and I didn't get the name for being small. I'm big. In my catcher's gear, real big. You can try going around me or you can try going through me. Neither is recommended. Ask Andy Herkert, who's got a bent nose to prove it. His sister Bev thinks it's funny. Andy doesn't.

But I'm way ahead of where I want to begin. So if you've got the picture of what I look like now, try to imagine me about one-quarter the size. Just get comfortable over on the couch by Grandpa and Mrs. B., and I'll roll this videotape of a picnic in the park one July when I was about seven.

That's me with the bat. Handsome little bugger, huh? Good stance, level swing. Yep, I had the makings even then. Waiting for the pitch . . . here it comes . . . and

1

...*am!* Heck of a hit. Good for an inside-the-parker, for sure. (No, that's not slow motion, damn it. I'm just not real fast on the bases.) Now see that little shrimp chasing the ball? That's Jeff Hanson, my best buddy. But catch that look in his eyes? That is one hacked-off little kid.

Okay, here I am coming home. A high five from Mom, another from Grandma, and back to the plate. Now here comes the climax. I'm set to really pound it this time. Jeff winds up, and . . . *Pow!* Did you see that? Just before the camera jumped around and the video went black? That little SOB plugged me! Stuck one right in my ribs. Sportsmanship, friendship, all out the window just because I hit a couple of his pitches. Well, let me tell you, Jeff hasn't changed one bit.

Jeff and I don't agree on a lot of things, and it hasn't always been easy being his friend. But no matter how mad he makes me sometimes, he's still my best buddy. Most of the time. We've hung together through some tough times. I stood by him when his dad walked out on his mom, and Jeff hardly spoke to anyone for months. And Jeff stood by me when my grandma died, and Grandpa and I had to keep going on our own.

But this isn't a story about divorce and death, but about how Jeff and I grew up playing ball. Because, you see, no matter what happened elsewhere in our lives, we always had baseball. We played on the rough field in the park from the time the snow melted in April to the time it came again in November. In the winter, we played catch in the gym or on the slippery walk in front

2

of my house. Other kids changed sports with the seasons, but Jeff and I were baseball players year-round. We practiced and played for the joy of it, but also for that summer day when we'd stand on the top of the dugout steps, waiting for our names to be called in a lineup filled with players whose cards we'd once collected. And we'd be like them at last, jogging smooth and easy to our positions while the crowd cheered and the sun washed across an afternoon as golden as heaven itself.

Sometimes that dream was so real that I could close my eyes and actually hear the roar from the stands, smell the infield grass, and feel the good hot stretch of my hamstrings as I crouched behind the plate, the pitcher's warm-up throws sizzling into my mitt. And when he stepped off the mound, his arm loose and his thoughts on the first hitter, I'd rear up to rifle the ball to second, feeling it leave my hand to blaze white-fire over the mound, to where Jeff, breaking from second, would take it knee-high to slap the tag on the imaginary runner. . . . God, I could feel it, every bit of it.

WINTER – SENIOR YEAR

"GET YOUR DOGS off the table, Neil. This is heavy."

I glanced up from the sports page to see Grandpa lugging a dusty cardboard box into the living room. I took my feet off the coffee table. "What's that?" I asked.

"Videotapes I shot when you were a kid."

I glanced in at the jumble of cassette boxes. "God, there's a fortune in tape in there. We gonna recycle 'em?"

"Hell, no. A lot of heavy lifting went into making those tapes. Camcorders weighed a ton back then."

He started digging in the box, and I went back to checking the basketball standings. The Bucks were in the cellar again. Figured. "Why're you messing with the tapes?" I asked.

"Ellen wants to see some of them tomorrow after

supper. Says it's time she learned more of the family history." Ellen is Ellen Barrens, Grandpa's very main lady for the last year and a half.

"Is she cooking or are we?" I asked.

"It's our turn."

"Bad luck."

"Well, we'll keep it simple. Spaghetti or something." He squinted at the label on a box. "Can you read this?"

I folded the paper and started helping him sort through the cassettes.

After supper the next evening, Grandpa put on a three-hour anthology of the best Larsen family videos. I wasn't thrilled about spending my evening watching home videos, but I wasn't all that enthused about going upstairs to work on my senior project, either. So, I leaned back in the recliner while Grandpa and Mrs. B. cozied up on the couch.

Grandpa started with an oldie: Mom's college graduation party in the backyard with a lot of people I didn't recognize and a few I did. Five minutes into the video, I toddled into the picture, clutching Grandma's skirt with one fist and sucking on the knuckles of the other. Mom knelt down beside me, smiling up at the lens.

Grandpa punched the still button to freeze the picture. "Ain't they a pair?" He grinned.

"Oh, they're just perfect!" Mrs. B. said. "Just look at Neil's pudgy little legs." Grandpa laughed and I grunted sourly. I was concentrating on Mom's smile. It was a great smile, a million-dollar smile, except that the warmth never quite reached her eyes. Even at twenty-three, this was definitely not a person to mess with.

Grandpa started the tape again, and we watched as I toddled along with Mom to get an ice-cream cone. When I had it clutched in my fist, I looked around for Grandma, spotted her, and wobbled over to get a grip on her skirt again. Mom went back to talking to the guests, leaving Grandma to clean up the mess I was making of my front and her skirt.

I didn't have to waste time looking for my dad at the party. Mom never told Grandpa and Grandma and she's never told me who knocked her up late in her junior year at the University of Wisconsin. (Personally, I think the guy's buried in a swamp somewhere. As I said, you don't mess with Mom and get away with it.) She came home, got big, and had me promptly on schedule. After that, she didn't waste a lot of time on sentiment. She bought a few months' supply of formula and diapers, told Grandma and Grandpa where they could reach her, and left the three of us to make do in Shipley while she went back to Madison to finish her degree. I haven't seen a lot of her since.

Grandpa changed tapes, and the seasons and the years rolled on. Mom had a bigger part in the tapes than she's ever had in my life because the camcorder always came out of the closet whenever she dropped in for a few days. While us rustics rusticated here, Mom was making it big in Los Angeles. Within days of hitting the Coast at twenty-three, she'd used her smile and her considerable smarts to get a job at a top public relations firm. Three years later, she quit to set up a PR shop with another "renegade feminist" from a big firm. (Her words, not mine.) Then, of course, she was busier than ever, and time went spinning along without her ever managing to find time to send for me. Before you know it, I'm nearly a teenager, Grandma's dying, and Mom is this big-time PR type with a few strands of gray in her hair. And nobody can figure out what the hell happened to all the time.

I'll give Mom credit for asking us to come live with her after Grandma died. But nobody was stupid enough to think it'd work. Grandpa said, "No, I'm gonna stick here. I was born in Wisconsin, and I guess I'll die here."

She looked at me. I shrugged. "There's nothing for me in LA. I'll stay with Grandpa."

I think I saw a twinge of pain or guilt cross her face then, but it was probably just the effort of covering up her relief. "Yes," she said, "that's probably best after all this time." And three days after Grandma's funeral, she was gone again.

Am I bitter? Not really. I've had Grandma and I still have Grandpa. Shipley's small, but it's not a bad place. I've got friends, a good enough school as schools go, and all along I've had baseball and my best most-of-the-time buddy, Jeff. Add it up, I came out all right.

"You're nodding off, Neil. Maybe you ought to turn in." I opened my eyes to find Grandpa and Mrs. B. smiling at me.

I stretched, glancing at my watch. "No, I was just thinking about something. But I really ought to take another look at my senior project."

"What's your project?" Mrs. B. asked.

"He won't tell," Grandpa said. "Big secret."

I got a Coke from the refrigerator and climbed the stairs to my room. I closed the door to give Grandpa and Mrs. B. some privacy and to spare myself the sound of groping and heavy breathing. Then, as I'd been doing for weeks, I sat at my desk and gazed balefully at the litter of printouts on my desk. What a mess.

The trouble began back in September when I asked Mrs. Wesley, the writing coordinator, if I could do a baseball journal for my senior project. She frowned at me over her half-moon glasses. "For this season? Baseball doesn't start until April, and you should be nearly done with your senior project by then."

"I kind of thought I'd write about the last two or three years. I've kept stats and a diary all along for fun, and I think I could pull them together into a pretty good story."

She thought it over. "Well, I guess that might work. I could use a break from the usual junk about when people were born, how much fun they had as kids, and why they're so miserable as teenagers. It's a bore."

I grinned at her. "Well, I'm a pretty happy person, Mrs. W. Especially when I'm playing ball."

"So I've noticed. You particularly seemed to enjoy breaking that boy's nose last year. Or was that the year before?"

"Year before," I said. "But that was kind of an accident. I forgot about the force-out at home, that's all."

"Was that it? Hmmm . . . Well, go ahead with your baseball journal, Neil," she said, pointedly not calling me "Bull," which even most of the teachers do by now. "Keep it lively and, for God's sake, try to spell things correctly."

"Let's see, t-i-n-g-z," I said.

"You're improving. Now get out of here and let me work."

I left her office thinking that I had my senior project half licked already. Wrong again, bozo. I entered my piddling diary into the computer and started filling in the gaps. But I could never seem to get to the point where I could say "enough," print out a copy, and hand it in. Perhaps it was because I didn't know the ending yet, and until we played this season, I couldn't make sense of any of it. And for some reason, that had become real important lately.

I finished stacking the printouts in order and paused to gaze out my window at the March drizzle trying to melt the last of the snow. Opening day was still three weeks away, and I felt as dull and soggy as the night. My final season — the season that would determine if I really had it in me to go any further in baseball. Jeff was going to make it, I was sure of that. A dozen scouts had looked at him last spring, but so far none of them had paid any attention to me. And that despite my tying for the league lead in home runs and finishing second in RBI's.

Downstairs, Grandpa and Mrs. B. started laughing at something on one of the tapes. She was good for him, especially now that I was going to be gone before long. Until then, I could put up with the comments about what cute, chubby legs I'd had as a toddler. I took a breath and turned over the first page of the stack.

SPRING —
NINTH GRADE

NGO HUYNH PHUONG. Mr. Keneally wrote the name on the board. "Class, I want you to welcome a new classmate. He is Vietnamese, and you pronounce his name 'No Win Fong.' Did I come close?" He smiled at the lanky kid standing near his desk.

"Close enough," the kid said.

"Good. Now, class, it's been explained to me that Vietnamese family names come first and given names last. So if the Bull over here were Vietnamese, he would be Larsen Neil, not Neil Larsen." I stood and made a bow just to make sure everyone remembered me. "Thank you, Bull," Mr. Keneally said. "You can sit down. So, class, you call our new friend Phuong, not Ngo." He smiled at the kid. "Right?" Phuong nodded without changing expression.

13

Keneally rattled on, telling us that Phuong's dad had been teaching at the University of Wisconsin medical school for the last few years and had recently taken a job at the clinic here in Shipley. Phuong had two older sisters in college and a little brother and sister at home. And a mother too, I guess, although I didn't hear much about her, since Jeff poked me about then.

"Will you look at that kid?" he whispered. "I thought all Vietnamese were short."

I measured Phuong against Keneally's six-two. "They must come in all sizes. He's five-ten, maybe a little better."

"And will you look at those arms."

I looked at Phuong's long, sinewy arms and big hands. "Big hooks, too," I said.

"You bet. That guy's our new pitcher."

"How do you know he even plays?"

"God, don't you watch the news, Bull? All those Asian kids are killer baseball players. Betcha he can hit, too." Jeff rubbed his hands. "This is the guy we've been waiting for."

Phuong took a seat on the far side of the room, and Mr. Keneally told us to get out our algebra books. I glanced at Jeff. He was already busy juggling the lineup card.

At lunch, we tried to get seats across from Phuong, but Sandi Watkins and a couple of her friends beat us to it. In a town where we don't see minorities very often,

Phuong was exotic and you could already see the girls maneuvering for a chance at him. I felt my usual rush of jealousy concerning Sandi.

Jeff caught my expression. "For God's sake, Bull. Didn't I tell you to forget her? She's only told you no about twenty times."

"More like fifty," I said. "Let me see that lineup card."

He dug it out of a pocket. "Way I see it, we'll be doing okay if I can play more short. We'll alternate Jim and Ned in right. Everywhere else we should be pretty solid."

"That's if this new kid can actually pitch."

"He can. I can feel it."

"And you're never wrong."

"Not when it comes to baseball."

I grunted. It was the truth, even if I wasn't going to tell him so. I glanced again at the table where Sandi and her friends were quizzing Phuong. He answered their questions, smiling slightly, but looking embarrassed by the attention. Fifteen minutes before the end of the hour, he excused himself, dumped his tray, and headed for the door.

"This is our chance," Jeff said. "Come on."

"I'm not done yet."

"Move it, Bull. You weigh too much already."

"Don't either," I said. But I followed along, balancing my tray in one hand while I tried to eat my pie.

Jeff glared at me. "God, you're slow. Give me that." He grabbed my tray, and I was able to slam-dunk the

15

rest of my pie before we headed up the hall to the class-rooms. Phuong was nowhere in sight.

We didn't find him until nearly time for fifth period. He was standing in the biology room talking to Ms. Heaton. She glanced up, saw us, and clutched at her heart. "My Lord, I'm having hallucinations. Captain Jock and Bull Catcher coming early to class." She looked at Phuong. "Are they really there?"

Phuong studied us without cracking a smile. "They seem to be."

"Are you sure? All the formaldehyde fumes around here can do funny things to your head."

Jeff grunted sourly, but I grinned at her. "We're here, Ms. H. Just thought we'd make your day."

"And you have, Bull. You definitely have. See that lab table? It's got to go to the art room, and you two look like just the guys to get it there." She gave us the dazzling smile that along with some pretty amazing chest development makes her the favorite teacher of every boy in junior high.

Jeff grouched. "Why do they need a lab table in the art room?"

She shrugged. "Lord knows. I just follow directions. *Di-rec-shuns*. They're sort of like orders. Like don't smash the doorjamb on your way out." She gave us that dazzling smile again. I melted; Jeff grumped. She went back to talking to Phuong while we wrestled the table through the door and lugged it down the hall to the art room.

Mr. Ferguson, one of the school counselors, grabbed Phuong right after biology, so we weren't able to catch him until after the last bell. He was headed for the door with about eight books under a long arm. "Crap," Jeff said as he dug frantically for the extra glove in the bottom of his locker. "You don't suppose he's some kind of brain, do you?"

I grinned. "Don't you watch the news? All those Asian kids are killer students."

"Don't make jokes; this is important. You know what they say, 'On the seventh day —'"

"God made baseball. Yeah, you've said that before."

"It's true. Come on, we've got to get this kid's priorities straight."

He jogged to catch up. "Phuong, I'm Jeff Hanson." He stuck out a hand. "Saw you around today. How do you like Wisconsin?"

Phuong raised his eyebrows a millimeter. "It's all right. I've been in Madison for the last three years."

"Oh, yeah. Right. I meant central Wisconsin."

"It's okay."

"Good. Glad to hear you're enjoying it. . . . So it must be tough starting at a new school in the spring."

"I can handle it."

"Well, good. So . . . " Jeff hesitated. "So, anyway, how'd you like to play some ball?"

Phuong stared at Jeff, and I noticed for the first time how dark and cold his eyes were. For a long second, I thought he was going to tell Jeff to buzz off, but then he said quietly, "Which kind?"

"Well, baseball, of course. We're getting geared up for the summer. Practice starts in three weeks. So, uh, what do you say?"

"I imagine I could give it a try."

"That's great. I think you're just the guy we've been looking for." He waved a hand at me. "Oh, this is the Bull. He's my catcher, and he's a good one. Can't run worth a damn, but he makes a real good target."

"Hi," I said. Phuong said hi back.

"Bull, scrounge us some gear from Keneally, would ya? We'll be at the field." He draped an arm around Phuong and almost dragged him toward the outside door.

I got the storeroom key from Keneally, who's officially our coach but doesn't do much except show up at the games, where he spends most of his time swatting mosquitoes. Jeff's the one who really calls the shots and that's fine with Keneally, who just agrees to be coach because his nephew Jim plays on the team.

Outdoors, it was your typical early April day in Wisconsin — cold and dreary. But the snow was gone and a wind was drying the soggy ground. I slung the equipment bag over my shoulder and headed across the brown grass for the field.

Jeff and Phuong were flipping a ball back and forth while Jeff talked nonstop. "You see, the problem is that I'm the only guy on the team who can really pitch, but

18

I'm also the best shortstop and I can't play two positions. What we need is another pitcher. When I saw those long arms of yours, I said, 'Whoa, talk about power. That kid's got it.' Now if you can play some outfield, too, and hit a lick now and then, we are going to be in fat city." He scooped up a low throw. "So, what do you think of the plan?"

"In theory or in practice?"

Jeff hesitated. "Well, in both, I guess. Hey, you speak pretty good English."

"I don't see why not; I was born in Los Angeles. And, by the way, I haven't played much baseball."

"No problem. I can tell you've got the skills. We'll just smooth out the rough spots. Bull, you ready?"

"Just about." I buckled my left shin guard, pulled my mask down, and crouched behind the plate. "Let 'er rip."

For a couple of minutes, it looked like Jeff had picked us a winner. Phuong wound up, and I could see that he'd played enough to get the motion down. And speed? Yeah, he had that all right. His first pitch came in like a BB and hit so hard that my palm stung through the padding of my mitt. His fastball had a natural tail to it, dropping just short of the plate and making it a little hard to judge. When I muffed his third pitch, it caromed off my right shin guard, and I began wishing that I'd taken time to put on my nut cup. I mean, Jeff's fastball was bad enough, but this guy's could make a steer out of the ol' Bull for sure.

Jeff yelled, "Come on, Bull. The rest of you is slow, but those hands are supposed to be like lightning."

I grinned, jogged after the ball, and flipped it back to Phuong. "It's got a nasty bite to it, partner. Give me another right down the middle."

While Phuong hurled and I tried to keep my Bull-hood intact, Jeff stood on the first baseline, grinning like he'd discovered the reincarnation of Nolan Ryan. But then Phuong lost it. He sent a pitch sailing four feet over my head, buzzing like an angry hornet. The one after that hit three feet short of the plate, splattering me with dirt. For ten minutes, I leaped and dove for pitches, but he never came close to the plate again. He still had enough stuff to throw the ball through a barn wall — but only if he were aiming at a pretty good-sized barn.

Jeff stood with his arms hanging and his mouth gaping as his dreams of a championship went through a nuclear meltdown right before his eyes. Finally, he set his jaw and marched to the mound. "Look, you're way overthrowing, Phuong. At the start, you just let the motion do it for you. Now you're forcing the ball. Let me show you." He snatched the ball from Phuong and sent three fastballs blazing across the plate to thunk into my mitt. He turned to Phuong. "That's how you do it. Nice and easy." He marched back to the sidelines and stood with his hands on his hips.

Phuong got the next couple of pitches close to the plate, but then everything went haywire again. I signaled for time and jogged out to the mound. But my lack of speed got me again, and Jeff was already laying it on Phuong by the time I got there. "Damn it, Phuong! Stop trying to blow a hole in the backstop. Just pick your spot and let the motion flow. The follow-through will give you the speed." Jeff pushed him away from the rubber and pantomimed a half-dozen deliveries. He let the ball go on the last one, and it zinged across the plate to rattle the chain-link backstop. "Now try it again," he snapped.

Phuong's hands didn't move. He fixed Jeff with a cold stare. "No, thanks. I've learned all I want to from this experiment."

"This isn't some science class! This is baseball. Now, come on, try to get one across the plate."

Phuong gave him a thin smile. "I said, no, thanks. I'll let you know if I'm interested in trying baseball again." He sauntered off to pick up his stack of books, leaving Jeff in a sort of paralyzed shock.

Jeff couldn't believe that anyone could walk away from baseball, and I had to give him a hard nudge to break the paralysis. We returned the gear to the storeroom and started for home. For a while Jeff slumped along in silence, then he did some groaning, followed that with five minutes of incoherent bitching, and finally fell to muttering to himself. He was still in that stage when we parted at the corner of Hayes and Grant.

Jim Keneally, Billy Collins, and I watched Jeff march over to where Phuong sat eating his lunch. Phuong

21

listened to him, shook his head, and went back to the textbook he had open beside his tray. And when Jeff went right on talking, Phuong glared at him, snapped the book shut, and walked out on him. Jeff came back to our table mad enough to chew razor blades. "Jerk," he muttered, grabbed his tray, and went to dump his half-eaten lunch in the garbage can.

Jim, who idolizes Jeff, looked at me. "Can't you do something, Bull?"

I shrugged. "Guy doesn't want to pitch, he doesn't want to pitch."

"Yeah, forget it," Billy said. "We don't need him. Jeff and me can handle the pitching. Bull says Phuong's wild, anyway."

Jim hesitated, not wanting to offend Billy, who's got a short fuse to go along with an ERA of about 14.79. "Yeah, but —"

"But nothing," Billy said. "Jeff said it, the guy's a jerk. Right, Bull?"

"The guy's got his own priorities," I said. "Leave him be."

But you can't say Jeff isn't persistent. The next day, he snapped at me, "You ask him, Bull."

"What difference would that make? He doesn't want to play. Leave him alone."

"He's just holding out."

"For what? A bigger signing bonus?"

Billy laughed and Jim giggled. "Come on, guys," Jeff

said. "This is important. I don't know what Phuong wants, but he's got to play."

"No, he doesn't," I said. "Only you've *got* to play. Most of the rest of us have a life now and then."

Jeff scowled, then tried to sound patient. "Look, Bull, maybe I broke some Oriental taboo and now the guy's not going to play until I do something to show him I'm really sorry. Just go find out what he wants. If I've got to walk over hot coals or let him stick bamboo slivers under my toenails, no problem. Just as long as it gets him to pitch."

"This isn't going to work," I said, but — as usual — I did what I was told.

Phuong glanced up from his book when I sat down across from him. "Biology?" I asked. He nodded and went back to studying a diagram. "Uh, Jeff really wants you to give us another chance. He said you can even stick bamboo slivers under his toenails if that'll help."

Phuong's head jerked up, and if his eyes had been cold before, this time they were black ice. He stared at me for a long moment, and then leaned back in his chair. "Doesn't that strike you as a racist stereotype, Bull? Something out of the *Rambo* movies where Stallone's always blasting evil little yellow men?"

Poleaxed. Yep, the ol' Bull had gotten one right between the eyes. And deserved it. I gave him a rueful grin. "Yeah, I guess it does. Hey, I'm sorry, Phuong. Jeff was just trying to make a joke."

23

"But you repeated it. And I thought you were the one with brains."

"Not this time, I guess." I hesitated. "I'll tell Jeff. I'm sure he didn't mean anything by it, either."

Phuong studied me, and then nodded. "Fair enough. But it's still no on the baseball."

"Phuong, I don't get it. The other day I could see that you'd done some pitching. Why don't you want to do any now?"

"All the pitching I ever did was in my backyard in Madison. I don't like teams."

"Why not?"

He hesitated, and for a second I thought he was going to tell me something. But he decided against it. "Because I don't. Now excuse me." He leaned forward, hunching over the biology text.

"Okay," I said, got up, and went back to our table to give the bad news to Jeff.

"Big Friday night plans?" Grandpa asked. He was standing in front of the hall mirror, knotting a tie slightly wider than a shovel.

"Nothing much," I said. "I might go over to Jeff's to watch a movie. He's baby-sitting tonight. How about you?"

"Figured I'd go over to the Eagle's Club for a while. See what's happening at the old folks' dance."

"Uh-huh," I said. "And who's going with you?"

"Didn't say anyone was."

24

"You didn't have to. You don't get this dressed up unless you're taking somebody."

"Well, Grandson, as long as you ask, I'm taking a very nice lady named Charlotte Fleming."

"Should I know her?"

"Wouldn't think so. She used to work at the bank. I knew her husband some before he died." He stood back to inspect himself in the mirror.

"Should I wait up for you?"

"No, I might be pretty late."

"How come? Those dances are over by eleven or so, aren't they?"

He gave me a hard look, which I returned with as much innocence as I could muster without laughing. "Well, Neil, you know what they say: 'Just because there's snow on the roof don't mean there's no fire in the furnace.'"

"So you've said. But, uh, there's not a lot of snow on your roof. More the red slate look."

"Now that," he said, "was uncalled for. Nasty, even."

"Just trying to fit the saying to the reality, Grandpa. No offense."

"Spoken like your mother's son. Shifty but smooth." He picked up the car keys and opened the front door. He winked at me. "Stay out of trouble. Don't do anything I wouldn't do."

"Now *that*," I called after him, "gives me a lot of leeway." He laughed and I grinned. My grandpa, the Big Swede.

While my dinner nuked happily in the microwave, I went out to sweep the shop. Grandpa opened his saw-sharpening business five years ago, when he retired from the Weyerhaeuser plant after thirty years of sharpening the big saws that milled the timber trucked into Shipley from the forests up north. The shop was just a hobby then, but after Grandma died, he added lawn-mower repair to get enough work to keep his mind off losing her. Soon he had more business than he really wanted. I helped out by sweeping the floor, cleaning and painting mowers, and hauling the trash out to the curb. Not taxing, but enough to keep me out of trouble for a few hours a week.

I practiced my trombone for half an hour and then spent an hour working on my mountain bike, which I'd been rebuilding since Christmas and hoped to have finished sometime before fall. Finally, when I was pretty sure Jeff would have the kids in bed, I walked over to his house.

A few years after Jeff's dad walked out, his mom married Gil Elsinger. Gil's a hell of a lot better guy than Jeff's father ever was. You can ask Jeff. Natalie and Gil got busy and now Jeff's got two little sisters. He grumps about baby-sitting, but I think he kind of enjoys it.

He opened the door. "Hey, Bull."

"Hi. The kids in bed yet?"

"Yeah, both down for the count. You should have come by earlier. Elise had the bad diaper of all time."

"Good training for you. You'll make a heck of a dad someday."

"If I'm ever that stupid. Come on in, I was just about to start a movie. Get my sex and violence fix after all this crap."

"So to speak."

"You got that right."

It was nearly eleven when we heard the garage door. Jeff flicked off the closing credits and glanced at his watch. "Five hours times six bucks an hour. Thirty bucks."

"You must have gotten a raise."

"Nope, that's just what they should pay me. I still get two bucks an hour."

"Good thing you enjoy it so much."

"Uh-huh. About like I enjoy algebra."

Gil and Natalie came in. "Hey, Bull," Gil said. "Keeping the noble number one son company?"

"His nobility is wearing a tad thin," I said. "I'm just here protecting the kids in case he loses it altogether."

"What time did you get them to bed, Jeff?" Natalie asked.

"A little before eight. Would have been earlier, but they decided they needed snacks. Elise had a gigaload in her diaper, but Sylvie was dry. So, she's probably wet by now."

"I'll check." She left.

Gil dug out his wallet and paid Jeff, who grumbled

27

that he ought to get time and a half for Friday night. It didn't get him anywhere. "I'm going to walk part way home with Bull," he said. "I'll see you in a few minutes."

Outside it was still warm, a wind from the south blowing a light fog across the drying yards. Jeff took a deep breath of the night air. He grinned. "Baseball weather soon."

"If you use your imagination."

"So, you think it's hopeless with Phuong," he said.

"Yeah, I think so. Might as well leave him alone. I don't think he's a bad guy. Just not into the same things we are."

"Well, to hell with him, then. Let's try the field tomorrow. Should be dry enough to do a little pitching, anyway."

"Sounds good. I want to see you work on that change-up some."

"Yeah. And you ought to do some wind sprints. See if you can make it to first in under a minute after all this time off."

"Hey, I'm going to be a burner this year. Just wait and see."

He snorted. "Yeah, that I have to see."

Not a lot happened for a week, while the spring warmed, the ball field dried out, and the grass started showing signs that it had survived another winter of subarctic cold. Jeff shuffled and reshuffled the lineup card, looking for a way to make us into a championship team. But without Phuong, we didn't quite stack up, and Jeff knew it.

Phuong stayed to himself — not unfriendly, just quiet. As we'd guessed, he was one heck of a student, a speed merchant in algebra and an ace at biology. But when it came to phys ed, he was a disaster.

The longer I watched him, the weirder that seemed. He had a ton of talent, anybody could see that, but it just never came together for very long. He'd make a couple of great plays in a volleyball or a basketball game and then mess up every time after that. It made Jeff mad as hell, particularly when Coach Renkins developed the habit of sticking Phuong on our team.

Everything came to a head the day we had phys ed outside for the first time that spring. Some juniors from the high school down the street were on the volleyball courts, just itching for a chance to stomp some kids a couple of years younger. And Jeff, of course, wasn't about to back away from a challenge. We gathered around him. "Look, we can take these jerks," he said. "We'll lull 'em a little, then rotate the tallest guys to the net and really stick it to them." He glanced at me and Phuong. "And, Phuong, for God's sake, keep your head in the game."

It worked — almost. With Jeff serving, Phuong and I came to the net and started putting some lethal spikes on the juniors. We were within a point of winning when Phuong messed up. Jeff set up the winning point a foot above the net, but instead of spiking it, Phuong swung wildly and missed completely. The juniors came roaring back, and we never got another chance at the serve. They laid down the winning point right in front of Phuong.

While the juniors cheered and high-fived, Jeff grabbed the ball and whipped it at Phuong. For once, his aim was off, and the ball went bouncing across the blacktop. Their stares locked — Jeff's blazing, Phuong's freezing — and I took a step to get between them. "Cool it, Jeff," I said. He glared at me, and then stalked off toward the locker room.

He was still furious when we stopped by our lockers on the way to lunch. Phuong came past, his usual stack of books under an arm. Jeff glared after him. "God, just look at him. Study, study, read, read. His eyeballs are gonna fall out."

I shrugged. "Maybe he enjoys it. I think I saw you with a book once."

"Knock off the jokes, Bull. You haven't been funny in weeks."

The ol' Bull takes some pride in the wisdom he subtly disguises as wit, so I shot back, "You haven't had a sense of humor in weeks. Not since Phuong decided that being Jeff Hanson's pitching machine wasn't the ticket to fame and happiness. Yours especially."

Jeff's face got red. "Is that what you really think?"

"That's what I think," I snapped, and walked away.

In the cafeteria, I sat down a couple of places from

Phuong. He glanced up and then went back to reading. I chewed my food, for once not tasting it. I was pissed at Jeff, pissed at Phuong, and not real happy with myself for letting the whole thing get to me.

Jeff slapped his tray down across from Phuong and sat down so hard that the dishes jumped. Conversation around us died. Jeff leaned in toward Phuong. "Hey, what's with you, man? I set up that ball perfectly, and you blew it. So we lose again, just because you can't concentrate for one damned second. *No Win*, that's a good name for you. Aren't you good at anything, Phuong?"

Phuong leveled that cool stare at Jeff. "I'm good at some things. Better than you, I imagine."

"Yeah, like what? And don't give me any garbage about math or science. I mean sports and games."

Phuong studied him. "All right, I'll play a game with you. I'll stare you down. No blinking allowed. The first one who blinks, loses."

"Well, no problem, friend. I've got more willpower in my little finger than you've got in your whole body." Jeff shoved his tray aside.

"We'll see," Phuong said. He reached into a pocket and pulled out a bag of sunflower seeds. "Ready?"

"Ready." Jeff leaned on his elbows and stared into Phuong's eyes. Phuong popped a seed between his front teeth and chewed the kernel slowly.

I kept time while maybe two dozen kids gathered around. It wasn't much of a spectator sport for the first couple of minutes, but by the time the second hand on the wall clock hit three minutes, I could see sweat starting to glisten on Jeff's forehead. Phuong seemed unfazed by the passing seconds, his dark, cold eyes never breaking with Jeff's burning blue stare.

At four minutes, Jeff's eyelids began twitching, and I could see him starting to breathe a little faster. Phuong popped another sunflower seed. Two more minutes edged off the clock. Jeff's eyes filmed, then started to tear. Phuong's eyes began to well, too. He smiled slightly. "The hardest part is letting a tear fall without blinking. I don't think you can do it. You'll crack first. Just like one of these seeds."

Jeff sucked in a breath through clenched teeth. "Not a chance, No Win. You're going to lose again."

Phuong cracked a seed between his teeth and smiled.

Minute seven must have been torture, but minute eight was agony. Jeff fought with everything he had, teardrops hanging on the lower eyelashes of both eyes. A tear slid slowly down Phuong's cheek. He didn't blink, only reached for another seed.

At eight minutes forty-three seconds, Jeff cracked. He dropped his face into his palms and rubbed his eyes furiously. Phuong sighed, straightened, and daubed at his eyes with a napkin. Jeff got up and stomped out, not looking back. Jim hesitated, and then picked up Jeff's uneaten lunch and went to dump it in the garbage can.

The crowd of spectators drifted off. "You won," I said.

"Yes, I won," Phuong said. He didn't seem very happy about it.

"Jeff will want to try again tomorrow. He'll practice in front of the mirror tonight." Phuong shrugged. I hesitated, then asked, "What's the deal, Phuong? How come you can't concentrate like that on volleyball or baseball?"

He looked at me, and his eyes weren't cold but pained. "I concentrate too hard, that's the problem. When I'm learning something, I do okay. Then I start wanting to win, and I concentrate so hard I mess up." He paused. "So then I make like I didn't care to begin with."

I knew exactly what he meant. More than once, I've stood at the plate with the crowd noise and the chatter from the benches pressing in on me and the whole game weighing me down like a load of sandbags. And the pitcher winds up, and the ball comes in big and fat, but I'm so tight that I can't get the bat off my shoulder to save my butt. Then it's strike three and I'm out of there, walking back to the bench with my head hanging, trying not to show just how bad I feel about letting the team down. But how could I explain to Phuong that sometimes it doesn't pay to think too much?

"But that's, uh, kind of a matter of practice. You know, getting comfortable with something. Then you don't have to concentrate so hard."

He shook his head. "I used to spend hours in the

33

backyard throwing a baseball against one of those elastic backstops. I can put a fastball just about anywhere I want to anytime I want to, just as long as nobody's watching. That's why I'm no good in a real game."

"Well, maybe if you explained things to Jeff. Told him that you just need some extra time to get comfortable —"

Phuong shook his head. "Not a chance. I'm *No Win* Phuong. I'm stuck with that."

I found Jeff down on the ball field. He was sitting by the first-base coaching box, throwing pebbles at the rubber at the center of the pitcher's mound. He glanced up. "Hiya, Bull."

"How you doing?"

He shrugged. "Okay, I guess." I sat down, picked up a pebble, and tossed it at the pitcher's mound. It bounced high off the rubber. Jeff snorted. "Hell, I've been trying to do that for ten minutes and you get it on the first shot. This is definitely not my day for competitive sports."

"You don't have a lot riding on this one."

"No. We don't have any ego thing."

"Yeah, I already know I'm better," I said, hoping to get a rise out of him.

But he was thinking about something else. "You know, I'm not sure I could stare him down if I tried every day for a year. He wasn't even sweating."

"But you're going to try anyway."

He shrugged again. "Maybe, I'm not sure. . . . God, what I wouldn't do to harness all that guy's talent. Those eyes would scare half the batters so bad they'd pee their pants. But what can I do? Phuong just doesn't care enough."

By now I knew different, but I couldn't think how to tell him. Finally, I said, "Jeff, I think you might try asking him one more time. But take it slow. Don't expect him to be a star right off the bat."

The bell rang for fifth hour, and Jeff threw a final pebble at the rubber. It missed. "He'd never do it," he said. "Phuong hates my guts, and I probably deserve it."

On the way to the door, I said, "I'm not sure, Jeff. I think you might be surprised."

Jeff sat down across from Phuong again at lunch the next day. Neither of them said a word all through the meal. Talk had gotten around about the staring contest, and I could feel the kids at the nearby tables getting ready to crowd in to watch the rematch. Jeff disappointed them. When they'd both finished eating, he leaned down and pulled his two gloves out of a paper bag at his feet. He tossed one on the table in front of Phuong. "We've still got fifteen minutes. Let's go play some ball." He started for the kitchen to dump his tray.

Phuong looked at me. "Do it!" I mouthed at him. He hesitated another second, and then got up and followed Jeff toward the door and the spring afternoon.

They threw the ball back and forth until it was time for fifth hour, and then did it again for nearly an hour after school. That was their routine for the next three days. They didn't talk, just tossed the ball back and forth. I watched from the sidelines, chewing on a blade of new grass and doing as much homework as I felt like. On Friday, Jeff said only one line: "Want to pitch some?"

Phuong shrugged. "I imagine I could give it a try."

Jeff shouted, "Bull, get some gear on. And try to hurry, Bull; we've only got four hours until dark." I bestirred myself but didn't make any rush of it. Let 'em sweat.

Phuong was fine for ten minutes, then lost it. But Jeff didn't say a word, and after I'd dodged a few nutbusters and scalp-shavers, Phuong started getting it back. He wasn't exactly in control, but maybe half of his pitches came somewhere around the plate. When he finally got three in a row over — all of them fast and with that nasty bite — I called, "Good enough. My legs are tired."

Jeff snorted. "Better get yourself in shape, Bull. We don't play many games this short." He turned to Phuong. "Team practice starts Monday after school."

Phuong nodded. "I'll see if I can make it."

Walking home, Jeff asked, "Think he'll show?"

"Yeah, I think so. But if he thinks too much over the weekend, he might not pitch worth a crap."

"Well, you deal with it. I'm going to cool it for a while. Let you work it out."

Mr. Keneally showed up for about fifteen minutes on Monday afternoon, just to be polite, and then left so we could get down to business. Over the years, we'd developed a routine. We did our stretching and calisthenics first, then ran some wind sprints before starting hitting and fielding practice.

With Phuong on the team, my routine changed. While Jeff got the rest of the team in shape, my main — almost my only — job was getting Phuong ready. I worked his pitch count up until he was throwing the equivalent of three or four innings every other day. He had his wild streaks, but you could see him getting more comfortable and more fluid all the time. It developed that he could cut the fastball to give us another pitch, and we started experimenting with a little lollipop change-up that was going to drive hitters nuts once he got it under control. And then there was my suggestion for a fourth pitch. . . . But I'm getting ahead of myself.

Phuong and I worked in the bull pen during fielding drills and through most of batting practice, before knocking off to get in a few swings against Jeff. As usual, Jeff came in tight and fast on me, but I could see him cutting his speed against Phuong. When I groused once, he grinned. "Temper, temper, Bull. You're just sore because I struck you out and then let Phuong hit a couple of easy ones." He slapped me on the shoulder. "Come on. We'll worry about his hitting and fielding later. Right now, all I'm worried about is his pitching. And that's your department."

The next Wednesday, while Jeff had the guys chasing fungoes in the outfield, Phuong and I moved from the bull pen onto the field. And from the mound, I swear Phuong could have drilled a Dixie cup. The other guys drifted in to watch. After a few minutes, Billy picked up a bat and headed for the batter's box. Jeff stopped him. "Billy, you've got more guts than sense. Phuong's not ready and neither are you. Wait a few days."

He was right. The next day, I needed a net to catch Phuong. Finally, after about twelve sprawls in the dirt, a half kilometer of chasing wild pitches, and three or four good dings on the shins, I signaled for time and trudged out to the mound without the vaguest idea of what I was going to say. Jeff, who'd been watching us between hitting fungoes, tossed the bat to Jim and walked out to join us. Phuong stood there steaming, so mad that he wouldn't even look at us. Jeff said quietly, "You just haven't got it today, Phuong. That'll happen. Come on, we'll go hit some fungoes." Phuong didn't move. Jeff hesitated, and then reached out and gently took the ball out of Phuong's glove. "Tomorrow you'll have your control back. Don't worry about it now."

"He's right," I said. "It happens to every pitcher. Even Jeff."

Phuong stared for a long moment into the distance. Then he sighed. "Yeah, okay. Tomorrow." He turned to follow Jeff, while I went to shed my gear and examine the bruises on my legs.

Grandpa was getting ready to go to the Eagle's Club. "How'd it go with your boy today?"

"He didn't have diddly. Maybe tomorrow."

"Well, it sounds like you've brought him a long way. Your mom called. She'll be in Chicago the end of next week and says she's going to try to come up for the weekend. So, you'd better figure to miss a couple of practices."

"I'm not holding my breath. She'll get overscheduled as usual."

"Maybe, but it sounds like she's really planning on making it this time."

"Well, that'd be nice. . . . Taking Mrs. Fleming to the steak feed?"

"Nope. She's visiting her son in Atlanta for a couple of weeks."

"The other women better watch out."

"Nah, I'm not on the prowl tonight. Might play some cards with the guys, though. Don't wait up."

"Never do."

I warmed some leftovers, swept the shop, practiced my trombone, and then called Sandi to get my weekly dose of rejection.

"I'm sorry, Bull. I've got other plans for Friday."

"How about Saturday?"

"Then, too."

"With anyone I know?"

"That's none of your business!"

"Sorry."

"Well, learn to take a no-thanks, huh?"

"Sure," I said.

"So, you making Phuong into a champion?" she asked.

"Working on it. He's doing okay."

We talked for another twenty minutes about this and that. More accurately, she talked and I listened. She rattled on about cheerleading, her role in the spring play, how she figured she'd make the honor roll again, what classes she planned to take in high school next fall, and so on, until finally she sighed and said she really ought to study.

After we said good night, I sat staring at the phone. Why was I such a damned fool? Her talking to me didn't mean a thing. Hell, Sandi'd talk to a corpse if she couldn't find anybody alive. Yet there I'd sat, heart aflutter with her every word. Love — what a pain in the ass.

As soon as I'd finished warming up Phuong the next day, Jeff yelled, "Positions, everybody." He waved to us. "You, too."

I stood and tipped my mask back. Somehow I'd expected this. I grinned at Phuong. "I guess you're throwing batting practice, partner. Ready?"

He gave me half a smile. "I imagine I could give it a try."

"Okay," I said. "One is the fastball, two is a cut fastball, three is a change, and four is the Ryne Duren."

This time he grinned. "Gonna use number four, huh?"

"Yep, and you know who's going to see it first."

For those of you who may never have heard of Ryne Duren, the great Yankee reliever of the fifties, let me give you two clues about pitch number four. First, Duren was fast as hell. Second, most batters firmly believed that he was legally blind. You guess the rest.

Jeff picked up a bat and stepped into the box. I said out of the corner of my mouth, "You'd better hope he's not wild."

"Don't I know it." He took a couple of practice swings, then shouted to Phuong. "Okay, hotshot, let's see what you've got."

"Get ready to duck," I said. I waggled one finger, and Phuong nodded.

Phuong's fastball came in belt high, and I swear it hummed when it dropped just before it crossed the plate. Jeff's swing was two seconds late and a foot high. Or thereabouts. "Jeez, does that fastball have a bite," he muttered. "Not bad," he yelled. "But I've got you timed, sucker."

He didn't — not by a long shot — and it took him five more swings before he managed to send a weak bouncer to first. He stepped out of the box while the guys fired the ball around the horn. "Nasty," he said. "*Real* nasty." He grinned like a wolf, and I knew that he was thinking about some unsuspecting sheep in a certain summer baseball league.

"Give him some time," I said. "He's not ready for the real thing yet." Jeff nodded and stepped back in. I let him see another fastball, then waggled four fingers. Phuong nodded, wound up, and sent the Ryne Duren screaming two feet over Jeff's head. Jeff bailed out with an audible yelp of terror. From his backside, he stared first at me and then at Phuong, who was doubled over laughing.

I grinned. "That's our new pitch. We call it the Ryne Duren. Like it?"

"Why you son of a — "

"Tut, tut," I said. "Temper, temper."

Much to my surprise and Grandpa's, too, Mom actually managed to drop in for the following weekend. At supper that Friday, she gazed at me critically and then turned to Grandpa. "Are you still cutting his hair?"

"Sure am, honey. Getting better at it all the time."

She harrumphed, something she picked up from Grandma but didn't do as well. "I send more than enough money for him to get a decent haircut every couple of weeks. He's shaggy."

"I thought that was the cool look in LA, Mom."

"Not in the circles I move in. You want to get someplace, you get groomed."

"Well, in the circles I —"

Grandpa interrupted. "We'll start sending him downtown. Seems a waste of money to me, but you're the boss."

Mom turned back to me. "And I hope you're wearing something besides blue jeans and sweatshirts to school. I'm going to go through your drawers and closet right after supper."

I made a face. "Well, okay, I guess. But try to keep my *Playboys* in order. They're under my socks, and I've got them arranged just right."

"Damn," Grandpa said. "Is that where you've been hiding them? You're supposed to share those, boy."

Mom gave us a disgusted look. "You'd better hope I *don't* find them." She set down her fork. "Well, I'm going to get started. It'll probably take me until past Neil's bedtime just to do the dresser." She left the room.

Grandpa and I started cleaning up the dishes. "My bedtime?" I whispered. "What is my bedtime these days?"

"Ten o'clock."

"You liar. She actually asked you?"

"Yep. She didn't think it was any too early, either. Did you go through your drawers like I told you?"

"No. I kind of forgot."

"Oh-oh. Well, we'd better hope that she doesn't recognize too much of the stuff she tried to throw out at Christmas."

"Dad!" Mom shouted from upstairs.

43

"No such luck," I said. "Sorry."

"Maybe she just found your *Playboys*. Do you really have some in there?"

"No," I said. They were actually down in the basement, but he didn't have to know that.

I'd planned to get in a little practice with the guys on Saturday afternoon, but Mom insisted on dragging me to the mall shopping. She hit me with the usual lecture on the drive over: "Now, Neil. I know that we don't have the most typical family. But just because I only see you once every few months doesn't mean that I don't care. And it doesn't mean that I don't have the right to decide how you're raised. You and your grandpa don't lack for money. I see to that. That's why it makes me just a little upset when I come home to find you two wearing clothes that would make a street person blush."

"They're not that bad," I said.

"They are pretty bad."

"Mom —"

"Don't argue with me every chance you get!" She glared at me, and I slouched in my seat a little more. She sighed. "Neil, I do not ask a lot. I really don't. As long as you help your granddad, keep your grades up, and stay out of trouble, I don't nag you. But I do think you owe it to yourself to look presentable. It's good practice for the future."

"Yes'm," I said. She glanced at me, alert for sarcasm. I looked serious.

And I really did want to cooperate, because I hated the fights we always seemed to have at least once a visit. But we hit three stores without finding anything that simultaneously pleased her and that I'd agree to wear. Which meant she was already in a heap bad mood when a couple of kids waved and called: "Hey, Bull. How's it going?"

Mom gave me a dangerous stare. "Are people still calling you that ridiculous nickname? I thought I told you to tell people that you already have a perfectly good name."

"I did, Mom," I lied. "It just didn't take with the kids. But most of the teachers call me Neil."

"Not *all* of them?"

Oh, oh. Mistake. "Well, all but a couple, and they're getting better. Just a slip once in a while."

"That's not good enough. I'm going to write the principal. This has got to stop."

"Don't do that, Mom. That'll just —"

"Don't tell me what not to do! You're my kid, remember?" We walked on in angry silence.

Fortunately, we managed to agree on a new suit in the next store. (I didn't wear a suit but once or twice a year, but if she wanted to spend the bucks, why should I mind if it hung unworn in my closet?) That made her feel better. She let me buy some shorts that I liked well enough, and we compromised on some short-sleeved shirts.

On the ride home, I said, "Mom, about the nickname

45

thing. School's almost over, and I'm going to high school next year. Up there, I'll make sure the teachers call me Neil."

"How about the kids?"

"Them, too."

She sighed. "I don't want to embarrass you, dear. If you promise to make a real effort, I'll skip the letter to the principal."

"I promise, Mom," I said.

"All right then. Now let's have a pleasant evening. Would you like to go out to eat?"

Sunday afternoon, Grandpa and I drove Mom to the airport in Mosinee. As always, she put on the teary act when she gave me a parting hug. "Be a good boy, Neil. I'll be back just as soon as I can."

I returned the hug awkwardly, sure everybody in the place was watching us. "Sure, Mom. Make the big bucks, huh?"

She turned to give Grandpa a hug. " 'Bye, Dad. You take care of yourself."

"Sure, honey. You, too."

Crossing the parking lot, Grandpa sighed. "She tries, Neil. She really does. But she's a big-city girl, now. The three of us don't talk the same language anymore."

"I'm okay with that. Always have been."

He slapped me on the shoulder. "I could use a beer, and I guess you could use something soft."

I shrugged. "Beer's fine."

46

"Not yet it isn't. Come on, we'll catch a quick one and then head for home."

On the last day of school, Jeff juggled the lineup card a final time. We were sitting in sixth-period study hall, waiting for word that we could turn in the last of our books and pick up our gym stuff. He grunted and then shoved the card over to me. "I'm going to start Phuong in right. He's faster than Jim and he's got a better glove. When he pitches, I'll move to short and Ned will go to right."

"How about Jim?"

"We'll play him when we're short a guy. I already talked to him, and he says he doesn't mind coaching third and looking after the equipment the rest of the time."

I nodded. Jim didn't much care if he played or not, as long as he got to hang out with the guys. And if his nephew was happy, Keneally was content to show up for the games to give us the coach we needed to be legal. "When's Billy going to pitch?" I asked. "He's no damn good at it, but he likes to."

"When we have to use him, I guess. If Phuong keeps coming on, that won't be much."

"Billy's not going to like that."

He shrugged. "We'll talk to him after school. Tell him that this is the year he gets to concentrate on his hitting and base running. He's not going to make the high school team as a pitcher, and he knows it."

* * *

The three of us walked home together. I'd expected to find Billy full of bounce and grab-ass, drunk with the possibilities of summer. Instead, he was grim with that rippling anger just below the surface that scared some people about Billy. Me included.

Jeff was focused on baseball and didn't pick up on it right away. "Billy," he said, "I think we'll make you into a reliever this year. Phuong is coming along and —"

"Do what you want. I don't give a shit."

"Billy's it's not that —"

"I said, I don't give a shit. I might not even be around this summer."

Jeff glanced at me. This wasn't about baseball. After a pause, he asked quietly, "Got some trouble on the grades, huh?"

Billy pulled his report card out of a hip pocket and shoved it at Jeff. I looked over Jeff's shoulder to see. Ouch. Big time ouch. Jeff hesitated. "Did you get screwed on anything? Anything you could talk to your teachers about?"

"Nah, I deserve 'em. I didn't think they were going to be this bad, but . . ." He gave a helpless shrug. "I just didn't do much."

Jeff closed the card carefully. "I'm sorry, Billy. That's rough." I made a sympathetic noise.

"In case you're wondering," Billy said, "Ferguson says I can still go to high school next year, but officially I'll still be a ninth-grader until I make up two credits."

"How are you supposed to do that?" I asked.

"Ninety minutes after school, three days a week. That's when all the really stupid kids like me get to make up credits since there ain't no summer school this year. Not that you'd ever catch me in some goddamn summer school. I'd rather die."

We began the slow climb that would take us to the top of McPherson Hill, where the statue of a Civil War general stared out across the park that bore his name toward a horizon shadowed with afternoon clouds. Jeff said, "Billy, Why don't you come over and stay at my place tonight?"

"What difference would that make?"

Jeff shrugged. "We could talk a little bit. Figure out how to tell —"

"Shit. You think my old man's going to listen to anything? He's going to take one look at my grades and then start pounding on me. Better not expect me to hit crap on Tuesday. I probably won't be able to lift a bat."

Billy's dad never hit him in the face, just again and again on the arms. I'd seen the damage a dozen times over the years. "Damn it, Billy!" I said. "You shouldn't have to take that. Just because your grades aren't so hot doesn't give your dad the right to beat up on you."

"Bull's right," Jeff said. "Come over to my place and we'll talk to Gil and my mom about it. There's got to be something we can do."

Billy shook his head. "Nah, that'd just make things worse. My old man'd kill me if I told anybody about

49

him knocking me around. I mean that, he'd flat-ass kill me." Jeff started to say something but thought better of it. Let Billy talk it out. After a minute, Billy went on, "You know, this time I really am thinking about taking off. To hell with him and this whole damned town. It can live without me, and I sure as hell can live without it."

Jeff glanced at me. We'd heard it a dozen times before, and we both knew he'd never do it. As long as Billy hung around to take the screaming and the pounding, his little brothers and sisters dodged most of the crap around home. And that made crazy Billy Collins the bravest kid I knew.

We reached the top of the hill and paused by the statue. Below, the park descended in sloping steps to the last few streets on the edge of the farmland that rolled on to a far horizon that General McPherson seemed intent on piercing with his stone gaze. "I've got to run," Billy said. "Really run. Bull, can you take my gym bag? I'll pick it up later."

"Sure," I said.

"I'll run with you," Jeff said.

Billy shook his head. "Thanks. But I gotta be by myself for a while."

Jeff hesitated. "Stretch first. You've been sitting all day." Billy obediently did a minute of stretching. "Billy," Jeff said, "if you change your mind, come by my place. We could —"

"Nah. Better to get it over with. Maybe he won't get

too pissed this time." He straightened. "We'll see you guys later." He loped down the grassy slope.

"I wonder how far he'll run," Jeff said.

"Until he can't run any farther," I said, and thought, or until his heart breaks.

"Crazy Billy," Jeff said. "Damn, there should be something we can do. His old man has got to be the meanest shithead in town."

"Yeah, Billy ought to talk to somebody."

"He won't. Back before Christmas, Heaton asked him if something was wrong when he came to class with his arms so beat up he could hardly hold a pencil."

"I don't remember that."

"I think you'd already left for LA to visit your Mom. Billy said that he'd just pulled a muscle. Heaton didn't believe it and took him into her office to talk. But he just denied anything was wrong."

"That'd be like him."

Jeff nodded, watching Billy's running figure disappearing into the shadows of the trees and reemerging smaller and then smaller yet again, as the hill fell away from under him.

It rained all weekend, spoiling two days of practice and leaving us only Monday to get ready for the opener on Tuesday. Phuong was almost bouncing with anticipation as I warmed him up for batting practice. For all of us, hitting had become an exercise in humiliation since Phuong had started throwing practice. But Jeff was letting him show his best heat until he'd worked through the batting order. Then Jeff would take over, giving the guys something they could actually hit every second or third pitch. But not too much; that he left to Jim, who could get them in the strike zone even if he had zip for stuff.

Billy stepped into the on-deck circle, dropped the weighted doughnut over the handle of his bat, and swung gingerly. He winced, and I knew for sure what I'd suspected since he'd come to practice in a long-sleeved shirt: his old man had pounded him good.

When I was satisfied that Phuong was loose, I walked out to the mound. "We're gonna work on your change against Billy," I said. "We'll heat it up against Ned and Jeff."

"The change? Billy will knock it all over the place."

I glanced over at Billy, who was still swinging the weighted bat in the on-deck circle, his face fierce with pain and concentration. "Don't worry about it. I'll explain later."

Phuong shrugged, and I went back to the plate. Billy stepped in. "How you doing?" I asked.

"Never better. Bring it on."

I held down three fingers. Phuong wound up and came in with the change-up. Billy swung under it. I tossed the ball back, held down three fingers. Billy missed again, ahead and on top this time. "Damn it, Bull. Quit with the lollipop shit. You're messing up my timing."

"That's what it's for." I tossed the ball back and held down three fingers. "Here it comes again."

Billy swung, and I heard him grunt with pain, as he popped the ball straight up. I flipped off my mask, took two steps to my right, and made an easy basket catch. Billy glared it me. "Fastball," he snapped. "Give me a goddamn heater."

"You can't hit a change when you know it's coming, how are you going to hit a fastball?"

"I'll hit it."

"The hell. You can hardly lift the damned bat." I pulled on my mask, crouched, and held down two fingers for a cut fastball.

Lucky I told Phuong to take something off, because his real heater might have broken Billy's arm. Billy swung hard, trying to get his arms extended, but the pain of the effort threw him off balance and Phuong's pitch nailed him in the left forearm. Billy yelped and went down. I knelt beside him, a hand on his shoulder, as he writhed in the dirt.

Jeff came sprinting in from short. "Let me see, Billy."

"I'm okay," Billy gritted.

"Let me see, anyway." Jeff laid a hand on his biceps, and Billy gasped. "Yeah, right," Jeff said. "You're just in perfect shape. Now let me see your forearm."

Grudgingly, Billy let him look.

Jim came hurrying up with the first-aid kit that Keneally had had made up for us in about his only meaningful contribution to the team in a couple of years. "I've got one of those cold packs," he said.

"Put it on," Jeff said. Billy started to say something, but Jeff cut him off. "Just do something sensible for a change, Billy. Okay?"

I'd forgotten all about Phuong and glanced up to see him standing a few feet away with Ned Greenlaw and a couple of the other guys. He looked stricken. "I'm sorry, Billy," he said. "I didn't mean to get it that far inside."

"It was dead center of the plate," Billy snapped. "It was my fault, so forget it. Go on and pitch. I'll be back." He followed Jim to the bench.

Ned said, "Let's do a lap, guys. Come on, Phuong."

Phuong looked at me. "Good idea," I said.

They started running, and I saw Ned match his pace with Phuong's so that he could explain what we all knew about the condition of Billy's arms.

"Damn it, Bull," Jeff said. "Why'd you let Billy try to hit heat?"

I snorted. "That wasn't heat, that was a cutter. His old man's messed him up so bad that he can't hit crap. We threw him three straight change-ups, and he couldn't even hit those."

Jeff compressed his lips. "Okay, I'm sorry."

"Yeah, you and me both." I watched Jim holding the cold pack to Billy's forearm. Billy was slouched over, his face gray.

"Well, we'll have to replace him at leadoff. No way he'll be ready by tomorrow," Jeff said.

"You think that's what's important, huh? Whether or not we've got a healthy leadoff man for the opener?"

"Don't give me a hard time, Bull. I'm just as pissed at Billy's old man as you are. I'm just thinking ahead."

I grunted, unconvinced.

The guys had made the turn in left field and were loping toward the infield. "Well, come on," Jeff said. "A lot of guys have to hit yet."

"What are you going to do about Billy? We can't ignore this."

"We'll talk to him after practice. See if he's willing to report his old man."

"If he isn't, maybe we should."

"You know that won't work, Bull. Billy'll deny anything's wrong, just like he did with Heaton back at Christmas."

I sighed. "What about Phuong? He's probably so shook he won't be able to get one across for the rest of the day."

"I think it's the horse and rider business. Fall off, get right back on." He leaned down and picked up Billy's bat. "Guess I'll see if I can hit that cutter."

"You're a lot braver than I am."

"Or a lot stupider. Tell me when you've got him ready."

* * *

Jeff, Jim, and I tried to talk to Billy after practice, but he wouldn't listen. Finally, Jeff lost his temper. "Damn it, Billy, for about two cents I'd call the cops myself. You are getting abused!"

Billy spun on him. "How would you know?"

"Because I've seen your arms. And what your old man does to you is called child abuse."

"I ain't no child."

"It's still abuse."

"You can call it anything you want, but it's none of your goddamn business. So back off!"

"Whoa, Billy," I said. "Take it easy. We just give a damn about you —"

"Yeah, yeah. Well, you can't help with this, so don't worry about it." He started away, then turned, his eyes full of a hurt so deep that I couldn't find the bottom. "Look, guys. I know you give a damn, and I appreciate it. But this is something I've got to work out with my old man. He's not such a bad guy. Really. So don't tell anybody. It'll just make things worse."

After a long moment, Jeff looked down. "Yeah, sure, Billy." Jim nodded and so did I. Billy turned and trudged up the street that would take him toward home. Or whatever four-letter word you wanted to call it.

The opener was an early game, and the stands were only a third full. Grandpa was there, and I spotted Mrs. Ngo and Phuong's little brother and sister.

The program director gave the usual speech about

the league's no-arguing-the-calls rule, told everybody to have a good time, and turned the game over to the umpires. Keneally handed the ump the lineup card Jeff had prepared, joked with the opposing coach for a minute, and then returned to the dugout, where he took his accustomed position at the end of the bench and looked around for a mosquito to swat.

"Play ball," the umpire shouted.

I'd been warming Jeff up in the bull pen behind our bench. "God, I love those two words," Jeff said.

"Me, too. Ready?"

"You bet. Let's go get 'em."

Their first batter was a lefty, and I gave the defense a scan to make sure everybody had adjusted. Billy, who was playing center, bruised arms and all, gestured for Phuong to shade toward the line in right. Phuong moved a few steps, and we were set. I crouched, put down the sign for Jeff, and waited for the first pitch of the season.

Jeff punched them out on two strikeouts and an easy grounder, and we were coming to bat. The opposing pitcher had diddly, and we got to him for five runs in the first. (I had a double, driving in two.) After that we coasted. We play seven inning games here, so we were six outs away and leading 7–1 when we came to bat in the bottom of the fifth. "Think your boy can finish up?" Jeff asked.

"Think so. Pretty safe lead."

"Okay, let's get everybody in, then. Billy, Dave," he

called, "you're done for the day. Good job. Cal, you go in for . . ."

Phuong and I went to the bull pen behind the bench. "Ready for this, partner?" I asked.

"I imagine I could give it a try," he said.

I hardly had Phuong loosened up before it was time for the real thing. I figured Phuong would be all butterflies, but he was fine. Better than fine; he struck out the side.

Our half of the sixth got long. I came up with two on, two out, and a run in. I'd been watching their pitcher and knew just what I wanted to see. I got it on the second pitch and felt that sweet shiver pass down the bat to my hands — that feeling like nothing else in the world. The ball rose high in the air, arcing gracefully into a descent to bong on the steel roof of the equipment shed forty feet beyond the left-field fence.

I rounded third, slapping Jim's hand as I passed the coaching box, and jogged toward home to shake the hands of my teammates. Sweet. God, it was sweet.

"First of the year," Jeff called. "Another dozen like that and we'll win the championship."

"You bet," I said.

Roary Chapman bounced out to end our half of the inning, and we went out to finish it up. But the long inning had given Phuong too much time to think, and we had to work at it some. He walked the first batter on four pitches and the second on five. I thought of going out then, but decided to wait another pitch or two.

Mistake. Phuong's next pitch was a good four feet outside, I dove for it, missed, and had to sprint after it. I scooped it up and spun to see their lead runner barreling toward the plate. Why you gutsy little bastard. Down ten runs and you're trying to score from second? I lunged for him, but he got down and slid a foot across the plate a second before I landed on top of him. I thought of putting an elbow into his stomach, just so he'd remember me for next time, but then I rolled clear to give him a break.

I called time and trudged out to the mound. "You should have backed me up at home," I said.

Phuong nodded, kicking at the rubber. "Sorry. I forgot."

"Well, no big damage. Okay, what can you get across?"

"Nothing. I've lost everything."

"How about the change?"

He shrugged. "Yeah, probably. But we can't just throw change-ups."

"Sure we can. We've got a nine-run lead, so we'll just let the guys play defense. You did fine last inning with your heat. Now let's just get the last three outs."

"You're the boss."

"Yep, and don't forget it."

I went back to the plate and started calling change-ups. It worked, and we got the next two guys on a sac fly and a liner to third. For the last batter, I decided to see if Phuong could get a heater across. No luck, and I went back to the change. The batter bounced the second one to Ned at short, who lobbed it over to Jim at first. Not a pretty inning, but we had our first win.

The guys gave Phuong the perfunctory congratulations the reliever always gets, and then we lined up to shake hands with the other team. The little guy who'd scored on the wild pitch gave me a sheepish grin. "Coach said I shouldn't have tried that."

"He was right. But it took guts. See you next time." I smiled at him the kind of smile that makes people a little hesitant to meet me up close and personal a second time.

Our guys took off, some going with parents, others walking home in twos and threes. Jeff suggested that we go downtown, but I said I needed to get home. "Well, I'll see you at practice tomorrow." He slapped Phuong on the butt. "Good game, No Win. First of a lot of them."

I walked with Phuong toward our neighborhood. "What's eating you?" I asked.

"Same old crap. I did fine until I started thinking too much."

"It happens. Don't worry about it."

"Well, I do. Next time I probably won't be able to hit a wall."

Oh, hell. I was tired and my legs ached. I took a deep breath. "Okay, let's go work it out." He looked at me, not understanding. "I mean it," I said. "Let's go practice until you can get a heater across."

He started to object, then nodded. "Okay."

60

It took us twenty minutes, but once he relaxed, the heat came in smooth and hard. Finally, I yelled, "Satisfied? My hand hurts."

"Yeah, I'm okay now." His eyes were dark fire under the ice. God, he scared me sometimes.

We played again on Thursday, beating another weak team 9–4. Jeff started, bringing in Phuong for the last three innings. Phuong gave up three walks, threw two wild pitches, and allowed three of the four runs. But he hung in there, throwing a mix of heaters, cutters, and change-ups until the last guy struck out.

That was the routine for the next couple of weeks. Billy pitched a little, with the usual results, and Jim finished a 15–3 blowout. But Jeff and Phuong did most of the work. Jeff gave him his first start in the third week in June. Phuong lasted four innings before his fastball went haywire again. We were already a run down, and Jeff didn't want to let the game get out of control, so he took the load and settled things down. Phuong took getting relieved okay. Pissed at himself, but not so that he couldn't bounce back.

Two games later, he got his first win, although that was largely thanks to some superb catching and two homers by yours truly. (Yeah, Jeff and a couple of the other guys had pretty good games, too.) The time after that, he was perfect until the fifth, when the other team scratched a couple of hits sandwiched around an error to load the bases with one out. Phuong hardly blinked, striking out the last two batters before giving way to Billy for the last two innings.

Grandpa thumped on my bedroom door. "Phone call for you."

I rolled over and pried my eyes open. "God, what time is it?"

"Seven-thirty. I've been up for an hour and a half. It's a young lady."

Sandi? "Okay, I'll be there in a minute."

I stumbled out to the kitchen and picked up the phone. "Hello, Sandi?"

"Hi, Bull. It's about Billy."

"What about Billy?"

"I saw him out behind school when I was riding my bike. I've made up my mind to do that every morning so I can lose a couple of pounds of flab."

"You don't have any flab. What was Billy doing?"

"He was out back on that flat place where they bring trucks."

"The loading dock?"

"Right. Anyway, he was all curled up in a corner, and I think he was crying."

"Did you talk to him?"

"No. I mean, he's kind of your friend, so I thought I'd come back and call you."

"Thanks, Sandi. I'll go over there right away."

"Hope he's okay. Bye."

I dialed Jeff's number. Natalie came on the line. "Hi, Natalie, it's Neil. Will you get Jeff up and tell him to meet me behind the school? It's important. Real important."

"Well, sure, Neil. Is something wrong? You sound kind of upset."

"No, no, it's nothing to worry about. Just, uh, something he'll want to see."

I ran for the garage and my mountain bike. Outside, the day lay gray and dreary, the streets wet from rain in the night. Grandpa was standing on a stepladder, pruning his apple tree. "I'll be back in a while," I shouted. He waved.

Billy was hunched up in a dry corner of the loading dock, hugging his arms to his chest. I got off my bike and approached carefully, almost afraid to disturb him. "Billy?" He didn't look at me. "Billy, you okay?" What a stupid-ass question. Of course he wasn't. I knelt by him.

"He started hitting me right off," Billy whispered. "Didn't ask me nothing, just started hitting. And he just kept it up. 'You lazy little shit. Pow. I don't know why I even bother to feed you, you lazy little shit. Pow. This time you're gonna remember what happens when you screw up in this family, you little shit. Pow. Because I am gonna make you remember, you lazy —'" His voice broke. "And I just couldn't take it anymore, Bull. So I ran. And I left Andrea and Davey and Sue there with him, Bull. And he'd been drinking, and, God, he had to take it out on somebody. But I couldn't stay, Bull. I just couldn't . . ." He started sobbing.

I put an arm awkwardly around him. "Billy, we gotta do something. We gotta talk to somebody." He shook his head violently, but I went on talking. "You can't keep taking this crap, Billy. It isn't fair. We gotta talk to the cops or a social worker or somebody."

"You don't understand, Bull. God, he'd kill me."

"No, he won't, Billy. We won't let him." I heard a bicycle brake behind me and turned to see Jeff, his face grim, climbing off his mountain bike.

He clambered up on the dock and knelt beside Billy. "Let me see." Billy shook his head. "Let me see, damn it!" Billy tried to unbutton his shirt, but he couldn't do it. He whined like a kicked dog and started to cry again. "It's okay, Billy," Jeff said, "I've got it."

When Jeff slid the shirt off Billy's shoulders and we could see his arms, I felt like puking. The bruises were a mottled red, shading to blue at the edges. In the middle of every one, a circle of bright red showed where Mr. Collins had driven his ring nearly to bone. "That lousy son of a bitch," Jeff muttered. "This time we're going to do something."

"No," Billy said. "I can't tell —"

"That's bullshit, Billy. Now you've got a choice: you talk to my folks or Bull's grandpa. Or else, so help me, I'm gonna call the cops myself."

"Jeff, I can't —"

"I mean it, Billy. We've been friends for a long time, but this time I'm not going to let you cover up for that rotten bastard. Now, choose, Billy. My folks or Bull's grandpa." Billy fought it for a couple of minutes, his face screwed up and tears running down his cheeks. "My folks?" Jeff prodded. Billy shook his head. "Bull's grandpa, then." Billy hesitated, and nodded.

Grandpa and I went outside while Jeff put ice packs on Billy's bruises. Grandpa was angrier than I'd ever seen him. "How long has this been going on?" he snapped.

"I'm not sure. A long time."

"Why didn't you say something?"

I shrugged helplessly. "We tried to talk to Billy a bunch of times, but —"

"Damn it. You should have told me. Or told somebody."

"I'm sorry, Grandpa —"

He waved my apology away and stared angrily into the distance. "All three of you," he muttered. "Ain't one of you has had a normal home life. So I guess you're just used to tackling things on your own. But, dagnab it, Neil, you are kids! You can't take on everything by yourselves. You don't know how." I stared at my shoes and then looked up to see him blink back tears. "God, that boy's arms," he whispered.

"What are you going to do?"

"I'm going to think. I know Jack Collins, and this could get nasty. I've always thought he was a bastard, but half the people in this town have bought cars from him and figure him for a good Joe." He frowned. "Who over at the school would be any help?"

I hesitated. "Ms. Heaton, our biology teacher, guessed something was wrong around Christmas. She talked to Billy, but he wouldn't admit anything was wrong."

"What's her first name?"

"Uh, I think it's Marjory."

"I'm going to call her."

Ms. H. was there twenty minutes later, dressed in jeans and a sleeveless top. Even in the circumstances, I saw Grandpa do a double take on her bust. It was something to notice, that's for sure. She stuck out a hand. "Mr. Larsen? I'm Marjory Heaton."

Grandpa shook her hand. "Glad to meet you. Billy's inside. Jeff Hanson's putting ice on his bruises."

"Have you called the police?"

"Not yet," Grandpa said. "We thought we'd wait for you."

"Well, I'll talk to Billy for a minute and then give Sergeant Hughes a call. He's a good man."

"Ms. H.," I said. "I'm not sure we should go to the police right away. Billy's real scared —"

"That's out of your hands, Bull. And mine. I'm a mandatory reporter, which means I've got to report incidents of child abuse or risk losing my teaching license. But, believe me, I'd do it even if I didn't have to." She went into the house. I started to follow, but Grandpa told me to pick up his tree-trimming tools since it had started to drizzle again.

A couple of minutes later, Jeff joined me. "How is he?" I asked.

Jeff shrugged. "How would you expect? Rough. Real rough."

"Ms. H. says she's got to call the cops."

"Yeah, I kind of figured we'd be heading that way. Once you get school people involved, they've got to do that."

"Old man Collins is going to give some people a lot of crap."

"Not as much as he's going to get."

"What happened, anyway? Why was he so pissed at Billy?"

"Something about washing the cars down at the lot. Billy thought he did a good job, his old man didn't."

"And that was enough of an excuse, huh?"

Jeff looked at me, irritation flashing in his eyes. "Spend a little time around a drunk, and you'll understand. My old man wasn't as bad as Billy's, but there were some things that happened back then that I can't even begin to explain. All I know is that booze gives some people all the excuse they need."

"I'm sorry. I kinda forgot —"

He waved a hand. "Forget it. That was a million years ago. It's Billy we've got to worry about now."

We worried, but that was about all we managed to

accomplish. Two policemen came, talked to Grandpa briefly, and then went inside. A few minutes later, the younger of the two came out, introduced himself, and asked us a few questions about finding Billy that morning and what we knew of his getting beaten up in the past. Like Grandpa and Ms. H., he let us know just how stupid we'd been for not telling somebody sooner. We nodded, feeling about as low as dog crap. He went back in, and a few minutes later, they left with Billy. Later that afternoon, they arrested Billy's dad.

By the Fourth of July, we were eight and two, and tied for the league lead with the defending champs from Caledonia, a little town about thirty miles from Shipley and just barely in the same county.

Off the field, the big news was that Billy's dad had agreed to enter a counseling program. Grandpa grumbled that it was just a way for the district attorney to get out of taking the case to court. Still, Billy seemed cheerier than he'd been in months. Maybe it'd work.

Sandi'd gone off to Maine for a month with her mother, and I was getting edgy without my weekly dose of rejection. So, I tried calling a couple of other girls and got lucky with the second — a certain Julie ("you can call me Julia") Roberts. I had to explain to her that I couldn't do that since Julia was also my mom's name, which opened up all sorts of Freudian angles that I wasn't prepared to deal with. At least not this early in a relationship. She stared at me. "Well, okay, then. Call me Julie. I don't care."

Despite that start, we had a few good, if not very serious times, before *she* went off on vacation for a month. Which left me back where I'd started. No girl and no social life. But, as Jeff said when I complained: "Forget it. Let's play some ball." And it was definitely time to do just that, because Caledonia was coming to town for the game we'd been dreaming about all winter.

I don't know what they put in the water in Caledonia, but year after year, they've got a dynamite team. We've played against them enough times to know some of the guys pretty well. Hank Lutz is a heck of a pitcher, probably the best in the league. Joe Spence, their left fielder, is about the only guy around who can hit a ball as far I can. And Gary Melcher, their second baseman, is a gutsy little fart who steals a base or two on me every time we play. (I like Gary, but one of these days I'm going to stick a ball in his ear when he's sliding into second.) And, since they're all bound to make the Caledonia high school team, we expect to keep seeing them.

Their bus was late getting in, so Phuong and I worked on his cutter for a few minutes. When we took a break, Jeff sauntered over. "How's he look?"

"Sharp. Real sharp."

"Good. Because I figure I'm going to do more good at short."

"So, you're going to let him pitch?"

"Yep. You see any reason why not?"

"No, except that I figured you'd want to pitch the mother of all games."

Jeff gazed for a long moment at Phuong, who was talking lazily with Jim and Greg Fowler over by the bench. "Phuong's better than I am. That's what counts. And, by the way, it hurts like hell to admit it."

"Well, you said it, all those Asian kids are killer baseball players."

"I don't know about all, but this one is." The Caledonia bus turned the corner and pulled into the lot by the ball diamond. Jeff gave me a slap on the rump. "Come on, we've got a ball game to win. Tell Phuong to relax and pitch his own game. I've got to tell Ned that he's playing right."

"Can we throw a Ryne Duren?"

"Think it'd work against Joe Spence?"

"Nah. Joe'd just laugh it off."

"Well, if there's nobody on, you can try it on that fat first baseman, Bruce what's-his-name. He hit two homers on us last time, and it might get him thinking. Otherwise, stick to the fastball."

"Gotcha."

For the first three innings, Phuong was something to behold. Except for the single Ryne Duren — which produced a satisfying chalkiness on one fat first baseman's face — I called nothing but fastballs. Except for one blooper to right by Hank Lutz, the champs didn't hit diddly as we scratched out a two-run lead.

With two outs in the fifth and a man on first thanks to an error by Roary at third, Joe Spence boomed one to center that looked like it might be trouble, but Billy drifted back to the fence, took a couple of steps in, and put it away. Joe jogged back to the dugout as I started stripping off my gear. "Cripes, Bull. Where'd you get that kid? I swear that fastball dropped a foot."

"Not quite, but it's got a nasty bite to it, doesn't it?"

"Yeah, it does. Tell him to throw me something easier next time."

"On your mother's grave, bozo."

He laughed, caught the glove thrown to him by Gary Melcher, and jogged out to left.

I was feeling damned good when I came to bat a few minutes later. Hank was still pitching, and I gave him a grin. "Dead center, belt high, Hank. That'll do nicely."

"No problem." He wound up and gave me what looked like a cutter down and away for a strike. Nice pitch. I stepped out, took a swing, and stepped back in. I figured he'd give me another cutter, a step up the ladder and still on the outside half, but he surprised me by coming in with high inside heat. I jumped back, my elbows out of the way. "Strike," the umpire yelled. I looked at him. Strike? Hank grinned at me, knowing he'd gotten a break. He tried to fish me with a ball outside and then another. No bite, friend. Two and two, and he'd come with heat. I knew it. And for the tenth time that year, I felt that sweet vibration down the bat. Hank said "shit" loud enough to get a warning look from the umpire, and I jogged around the bases, my feet hardly touching the ground.

With a three-run lead and Phuong pitching like Nolan Ryan, I figured we'd have the game in the bag if we could get through the sixth. But leading off, Gary Melcher dribbled a single into center. Hank tried to bunt for a hit but stepped into a Phuong heater. (Luckily, it took him on the thigh, and he managed to stagger down to first.) That was enough to shake up Phuong. Bruce, the fat first baseman, stepped in, still looking a little chalky. I put down one finger and set up dead center of the plate, but Phuong's pitch was a yard outside. I dove for it and spun to see Gary sliding into third. Damn him, anyway. One of these days . . .

I called time and jogged out toward the mound. Jeff started in from short, but I waved him back. On our bench, Keneally roused himself long enough to give me an inquisitive look. I let him have a reassuring grin.

Phuong was glaring at his shoes, glove on hip. Before I could say anything, he muttered, "It's going to happen again."

"Horse crap!" I snapped, jolting him into looking at me. I grinned and drawled it out slow: "Horrrse craaap. I'm going to put up my mitt and you're going to hit it. That's all I'm going to do and that's all you have to worry about."

"And you seriously think that's going to work?"

"Guaranteed, partner. We're just gonna play catch."

He took a deep breath. "Okay. Just a game of catch."

I gave him a swat on the butt and jogged back to the plate. I grinned at fat Bruce. "Seen any good emergency rooms lately? My boy's gone just a tad wild." Bruce didn't think it was funny. Nor did the next guy or the guy after him, as Phuong struck out the side.

We didn't add any runs in our half of the inning, but I knew it didn't matter anymore. Phuong came out for the top of the final inning with his eyes cold as black ice. He was in the zone so far that I don't think he even heard the fans in the stands giving him a standing O.

I glanced out at Jeff, who was nervously kicking the dirt at short. I knew that he was dying to call time for a quick visit to the mound, but he managed to control himself. Phuong mowed down the first two batters like they were little kids swinging sponge bats. And that put him against Joe Spence for the final out.

As Joe made his way to the batter's box, I glanced again at Jeff. He was actually gnawing on the trailing end of a rawhide lace on his glove. I smiled and turned my attention to Joe. This time, he didn't make any jokes. He stepped into the box, got in his crouch, and waited. I put down a single finger, set up outside, and watched Phuong's fastball sing past Joe's swinging bat. Joe grunted, moved a half step back in the box, and waited. Phuong nipped the inside corner for a called strike. And Joe knew it. He stepped out — something he almost never does — took a few deep breaths, and stepped back in. "Bring it on," he growled.

I put down one finger, set up middle of the plate, and watched Phuong's pitch come singing straight down the pipe. And Joe couldn't catch up to it. The umpire's hand came up in the clenched fist. "Out and game," he yelled. Jeff's self-control broke and he charged for the mound.

When I got there a minute or two later — my speed hadn't improved any since spring — Jeff was thumping Phuong on the back and yelling: "No Win Phuong! That's what everybody's going to call you now, because nobody's ever gonna win against you again."

About that time, all the other guys got to the mound, and there was a lot of backslapping and high-fiving. In the middle of it all, Phuong just grinned. And for once his eyes weren't a bit cold. I winked at him. "You've got yourself a team," I said, and handed him the ball. "Have 'em autograph it."

WINTER –
SOPHOMORE
YEAR

I WISH I COULD TELL YOU that we went on from there to crush every team we played on our way to winning the league championship. But three days after the game against Caledonia, a dog ran out in front of Jeff when he was doing about thirty on his mountain bike on the downhill past McPherson Park. Jeff missed the dog but not the curb and, according to what he recollects, did a two-and-a-half gainer before hitting the sidewalk. Three cracked ribs, one broken wrist, and no baseball for the rest of the summer. But, as the doctor told him, it might have been the rest of his life if Gil and Natalie hadn't insisted that he wear a helmet. (The accident made a for-sure believer out of me.)

It might have been easier on the rest of us if Jeff had spent the rest of the season in a coma. He spent the games prowling the sidelines, yelling instructions and trying through sheer will to make us a championship team. But without him, we weren't close. We finished fourteen and eight, a distant third behind Caledonia and Lein's Forks.

This story is supposed to be about baseball, so I won't waste a lot of time describing the off-season. The day after the last game, Grandpa and I flew to California. Mom took off time to take us to Yosemite and Death Valley, although I don't think an hour passed that she wasn't on her cellular phone. Then it was time for the usual farewells and her promise of a long visit at Christmas, when we'd also celebrate my sixteenth birthday.

The day after Labor Day, Jeff, me, and the guys made it to the big time at last: Shipley Consolidated High School. A lot of the guys we'd played against in summer league would now be our classmates and maybe even teammates come spring. But not, unfortunately, the guys from Caledonia or Lein's Forks.

Jeff runs cross-country in the fall, more to stay in shape than for the competition. (Or so he says.) Coach Fredericks wanted me to try out for the jayvee football team. But Grandpa said, "I'd rather you stuck with the trombone," and Mom said, "No football, positively, absolutely, unequivocally not," which finished off that possibility. So, I signed on with the Hornet marching band.

Sandi had, of course, become one of the stars of the incoming sophomore class: captain of the jayvee cheerleading squad, romantic lead in the fall musical, and a major heartthrob and sexual fantasy for an exceedingly high percentage of the male population of the school. (Not exactly a big change there.) I was, of course, still stupid enough to be in love with her.

When basketball season rolled around, Jeff and I signed on to one of the intramural teams. Since we only practiced once and played once a week, we had a lot of time left over for keeping our baseball skills sharp. Every other day we worked with weights and then jogged or swam before getting out the gloves and heading for the mezzanine above the equipment rooms. At least one evening a week — and more when we could afford it — we'd hit in the batting cage at the sports center downtown, where Willie-Boy Parker, the best one-legged hitting instructor in the hemisphere, gave us free advice and only occasional abuse.

Did anything concern me besides sports? Sure. Sometimes, anyway. It was a beautiful fall, and Grandpa and I went sturgeon fishing. Grandpa takes his fishing seriously, but I really don't care if I land anything or not. It's just good to be outdoors before the long winter.

I enjoyed classes about as much as I usually did — say, half the time. At semester, I had my usual A's and B's, which satisfied me, even if they only just satisfied Mom. At Christmas, she bitched some about my clothes but liked the carpeting she'd ordered for the living room. Over dinner the second night, Grandpa had guts enough to ask her if she was seeing anyone special. "Nobody that special. I don't have time." She looked at him hard. "And how's your social life, Dad?"

Grandpa, whose look of innocence wouldn't fool a blind goat, said, "That's it, honey. Just social. Nothing more."

She snorted. "I'll bet. I just hope all your women friends are beyond the reproductive age. I do not make enough money to start settling paternity suits."

"Whoa," I said. "Aren't we forgetting those present of tender years and big ears?"

She set down her fork in one of those decisive gestures I'm sure they teach in PR school. "Speaking of which, maybe you and I ought to have a talk about some things."

I probably paled at that possibility, but she never carried through on her threat. Once she was safely back in LA, Grandpa went on with his social whirl of Eagle's Club dances, steak feeds, and card and bingo nights. My social life was duller, despite my new driver's license. Gwen Schmidt asked me to the Job's Daughters dance, and we went out once or twice a week for a couple of months before we started having certain communication difficulties on the subject of sports. At least I gathered that was the issue when she said: "You know, I might hold out some hope, except that you're already going steady with Jeff Hanson."

"Huh?" I said.

"Ah, forget it."

"No, what do you mean?"

"Well, it's just that you guys are always playing baseball or getting in shape to play baseball or talking about baseball or doing something with baseball. God, don't you guys ever get tired of *baseball*?"

"No," I said truthfully, and she groaned.

Still, I liked Gwen. So, the next day I asked Jeff's advice. He listened for a minute or two, and then said, "Come on, you can tell me the rest while we're playing some ball." And somehow, by the time we'd climbed to the mezzanine, the question of whether Jeff and I did or did not spend too much time on baseball no longer seemed important. Of course we didn't.

Then finally, just when there didn't seem much hope that the snow would ever melt, spring made some faint twitchings of life. Jeff, who's tuned into that sort of thing better than any groundhog, immediately perked up, sniffed the air, and grinned. "Did I ever tell you that on the seventh day — "

"God made baseball. Yeah, you mentioned that before."

"It's true."

SPRING — SOPHOMORE YEAR

"HOLD IT RIGHT THERE, HANSON!"

Jeff stopped halfway to the mound to stare at Coach Borsheim. "Uh, Coach, I just wanted to tell Phuong —"

"I don't care what you wanted to tell him! Around here, I do the telling. Now get back to your position or get off my field."

A couple of the seniors on the bench laughed and then shut up when Borsheim shot them a glare. "You ready, Larsen?" he asked me.

"Yes, sir," I said, and crouched behind the plate as he stepped into the box. I hesitated. "Anything in particular you want to see, Coach?"

"Just straight stuff. We're going to see who's got what for speed."

"Yes, sir," I said, and put down two fingers for a cutter. Phuong nodded and went into his windup. The ball came in straight and true, dipping just before it crossed the plate to drop under Borsheim's swing. He glanced at me sharply. "I said straight stuff."

"All his hard stuff works that way, Coach. Don't ask me how he does it, but it all has a bite to it."

Borsheim grunted and leveled his bat again. Phuong leaned in for the sign. I called another cutter. Borsheim slapped it to short, where Jeff picked it clean and rifled it to first. "That wasn't a fastball," Borsheim said. "That was a cutter."

"Yes, sir."

"Let me see his best."

"Yes, sir." I held down one finger, praying that Phuong wouldn't lose his control. Borsheim looked twenty pounds too heavy and ten years too old to get out of the way of a Phuong-ball gone wild. Phuong nodded and let 'er rip. And, no surprise, Borsheim missed by a foot.

"Hanson, Walters," he yelled. "What the hell are you doing?" Jeff was nearly behind second, while Terry Walters, a pretty good second baseman who'd batted against Phuong a dozen times in summer league, had swung way over toward first. They glanced at each other. "Well?" Borsheim yelled.

"Uh, just anticipating where you're likely to hit a fastball, Coach," Jeff called.

He glared at me. "Did you move them?"

I guess I should have lied. After all, Jeff and I thought

82

so much alike by now, I really didn't have to tell him where to play. But instead I said, "No, sir."

"Okay, Hanson, get off the field! On my teams, I set the defense. And I do it through the catcher. Now go sit on the bench and think about that, young man."

Ordering Jeff off a baseball diamond is like ordering a normal person to stick an important piece of anatomy into a garbage disposal. But he went. Charlie Worth, a junior infielder, jogged in to take his place.

Borsheim fouled off the next pitch and missed two more heaters before he finally managed to chop one over second about a yard to the right of where Jeff had been playing him. Nobody commented. Billy scooped it up in shallow center and lobbed it to Terry. Borsheim yelled, "Put some mustard on it, Collins." Billy waved and jogged out to medium center. Borsheim looked at me. "So this is the great No Win Phuong everybody talks about?"

"Yes, sir."

"You been catching him for a while?"

"Just last summer."

"Well, he's a keeper."

"Yes, sir."

"Halloway," he yelled. "Come and have a look at this kid. You're going to be catching him a lot. The rest of you varsity gather around Coach Haight and then we'll see if you can hit this kid's stuff." He turned to me again. "How's his curve?"

"We just started working on it, so it's not much yet. But he's got a good change."

"To win in this league, he's going to need a curve. A good one."

"Yes, sir."

He walked off toward the dugout, where Mr. Haight, the assistant coach, was calling out the names on the day's hitting roster. Wes Halloway, the big senior catcher and team captain, came over, adjusting the strap on his mask. Wes had been all-conference the year before, which meant he didn't have to worry about his job and was easier to get along with than a lot of the guys on the varsity. Rob Patzwald, a junior, was his backup, making me the scrub who'd catch most of the jayvee games. "How's your boy look?" Wes asked.

"Super," I said. "Fastball's biting a good four inches."

"What happens if I call a deuce?"

"God knows. I sure wouldn't want to stand in against a Phuong curve until he gets better control of it."

"Well, we'll stay away from it then . . . Damn it. What's wrong with this strap?" He gestured at Phuong. "Stay loose. Play some catch with first." He went back to straightening out the strap. "I'm going to let you do the work with him on the curve. You discovered him, and you'll have a lot of time in the bull pen with him."

For a second that didn't register. "How about Patzwald?"

"Patz quit this morning. Thought about the double and the homer you hit in scrimmage yesterday and said to hell with it. Told Borsheim he's not spending another year backing me up just so he can waste next year playing behind you. Besides, he's got a good job after school. So, congrats, you're my backup."

"Thanks," I said. "I'm deeply honored and all that shit."

"You oughta be." He glanced toward the bench where the varsity had gotten their instructions and were selecting bats and pulling on batting gloves. "By the way," Wes said, "you'd better teach your buddy Hanson some smarts. You don't know this new coach yet, but some of us got a good dose of him back in the fall when he coached linebackers. Believe me, he definitely takes no shit."

"I kinda figured that out."

"Well, I didn't think you were stone stupid, even if you are a rookie. But by the way, Borsheim also knows his baseball. Well, here we go." He put on his mask. "Okay, ace," he called to Phuong. "Give me a couple before we start working on these turkeys."

I went to the bench to take off my gear. Jeff looked up. "Sure you want to sit by me?"

"Don't be stupid."

"I'm not sure I'd sit by me if I had a choice."

I shrugged out of my chest protector and sat beside him to take off my shin guards. "Borsheim's just riding you a little. You're too damned good to cut. He knows that."

"Yeah, right — Hey! Nice catch, Billy!"

Billy had galloped into shallow right center to pick a sinking liner off his shoe tops. I clapped a couple of times, about all I felt like doing for one of my less favorite people these days. "So," Jeff said, "I heard a couple of the seniors say Patz quit."

"Yeah, Wes just told me."

"Means you're number two and on the varsity."

"Not officially."

He snorted. "What else is Borsheim going to do? If Wes couldn't play, he'd probably jump you ahead of Patz anyway."

I looked at him with irritation. "Did it ever occur to you that maybe I'd rather catch every game for Haight and the jayvees than sit around warming up pitchers and watching Wes Halloway win all-conference again?"

"No," he said. "And it didn't occur to you, either."

I almost lost my temper with him then, but Jeff didn't need that. This was the third time in a week that Borsheim had benched him to "think" about something. In a month of conditioning, indoor drills, and now outdoor practice, Jeff had fallen nearly to the bottom of the depth chart for infielders. And all because he couldn't keep from stepping on Borsheim's toes. Now, barring a catastrophe that would kill or maim at least half a dozen guys ahead of him, Jeff wasn't even going to start for the jayvees, much less make the varsity.

I tossed my shin guards under the bench and settled back to watch Phuong work through the varsity lineup. It was slow going, each of the guys taking half a dozen rips and Borsheim stopping the action to give ill-tempered advice on stance and swing. Wes had slowed Phuong down, and they appeared to be using a mix of cutters and change-ups, moving things around and experimenting with different speeds. They worked well together, and I felt a twinge of jealousy, though nothing like the one I was about to feel.

Behind us, bike brakes squeaked. "Hi, Bull. Hi, Jeff. How's Billy doing?"

I turned to stare through the chain-link fence at Sandi. She was a little breathless from the ride, her cheeks glowing in the April sunshine. I managed to control my voice. "Hi, Sandi. He just made a nice catch."

She grinned, tossing back her hair and giving a little cheerleader jiggle of her torso. "That's my guy."

"Uh-huh," I said.

When the last varsity player had taken his quota of swings and circled the bases, Borsheim sent the starters in to play defense and brought Glen Anderson in to humiliate the rest of us. And as proud as I was of Phuong, I had to admit that Glen was still the ace, what with his control, a big roundhouse curve, and some very respectable heat.

Billy avoided looking at me when he jogged in to the bench. He whispered with Sandi for a couple of minutes, took a glance to see if Borsheim was watching, and kissed her quick through the fence. "I'll see you later," he said.

"Love ya," she said.

I got to the plate ready to take out everything on the ball. Wrong attitude. Glen struck me out with two curves and a change-up, and then a second time with a curve, a change-up, and another curve. I stepped out and looked at Borsheim. "You're not getting out of there until you at least touch something, son. Unless you'd rather take your shower at home."

I stepped back in. But as I tried to adjust to the slow stuff, Glen started coming at me with heat. Strike one. (Or seven, if you were counting from the beginning.) Hard curve off the outside corner. Ball. Heat again. Strike two.

I stepped out, breathing hard, my hands shaking. I took a practice cut, careful not to look at Borsheim, and stepped back in. "Deuce," Wes whispered. "Dead center."

I got it all. Out in left, Bob Ronchetti loped a few cosmetic steps toward the fence and then watched it go. Standing beside me, Wes said, "Woo-eee. And it didn't come down till the Fourth of July. By the way, Coach is waving for you to run the bases."

I jogged around the bases, slowing to a walk as I touched home. "I owe you one," I muttered to Wes.

"Yep. And don't think I'm gonna forget it."

Sandi was gone, had probably left while Glen was still tying me in knots with his curve. Maybe that shouldn't have made any difference to me, but it did. I took the fives and handshakes from the other guys, including Billy, and then sat brooding at the end of the bench. Why the hell was Sandi going out with Billy of all people? I couldn't figure it, and I'd even been sore-head enough to ask.

"Bull!" she'd yelped. "That's none of your business. Besides, what difference does it make to you?"

"You know damn well what difference. Come on, what's the deal?"

"Well, why shouldn't I go out with Billy? He's hand-some, he's smart —"

"Smart? He barely made it to high school this year."

"So he got some bad grades. That doesn't make him dumb. Hey, I thought you two were friends."

"So did I. I just learned different."

"Don't you go blaming him, Bull. And don't you blame me, either. I like Billy and he likes me. He makes a girl feel needed."

I snorted. "What are we talking about here? Mothering?"

There was a long pause on her end of the line, and I knew that I'd really stepped in it this time. But before I could think of a way to lighten things up, she said evenly, "Bull, that was mean, unkind, and rude. I don't think you ought to call me anymore."

"Hey, look, I'm sor —" I was talking to dead air.

Batting practice was nearly over, and Jeff moved hesi-tantly to the on-deck circle. When the batter ahead of him had taken his cuts, he looked at Borsheim, who stared back for a long moment before gesturing him to-ward the plate.

Wes didn't have to tip him, because Jeff was zoned in from the first pitch. He slashed one to left, then one to right, and then to prove he could spray it anywhere he wanted to, cracked one over second into center. All clothesline singles, the kind of hits that win ball games.

"All right, men," Borsheim yelled. "Once around the outfield and then hit the showers. Hanson and Larsen, two extra laps."

"What the hell did I do?" I panted when we were halfway through our second lap.

"Sat by me," Jeff said.

"Oh, horse crap."

"You think so, huh?"

"Yeah, I do."

"Well, keep thinking it. Me, I'm gonna give up thinking as a bad habit. From here on in, I'm doing everything Borsheim tells me to and not a damn thing he doesn't."

Maybe that wasn't such a bad plan. God knows, nothing else had worked. We jogged past the bull pen. Jim Keneally, who'd taken the job of bull pen manager, grinned and waved to us. We gave him the finger. "I still want to know what I did to get these laps," I said.

"Maybe he's trying to speed you up," Jeff said. "Come on, pick 'em up, Bull, I'm barely jogging."

"Careful," I said. "You're starting to coach again."

* * *

I was in my street clothes when Wes called, "Hey, rook. Coach wants to see you."

Borsheim didn't look up when I stood in front of his desk. "Larsen, don't you ever stand at the plate and watch one of your homers go. You know why?"

"Uh, yes, sir."

"Why?"

"Well, the wind could hold it up so it dropped in the field of play. Then I'd really have to push it to make second."

"And you're no burner to start with."

"No, sir."

He put down his pen and leaned back, staring at me. "Do you know an even better reason?"

"Uh, yes, sir. Because you told me not to."

"You're getting it. Because no matter what young Mr. Hanson thinks, this is not a democracy. We don't have two or nine or twenty-five head coaches. We've got one. And you know who he is."

"Yes, sir."

"Good. So, I imagine you heard that Patzwald quit."

"Yes, sir."

"And, I imagine you're expecting to be number two behind Halloway."

How the hell was I supposed to answer that? If I said, "Yes, sir," he'd land on me for being cocky. If I said, "I hadn't thought about it," he'd know I was lying. I met his eyes. "I can do the job, Coach."

He raised his eyebrows. "Good answer. Halloway told me you're brighter than the average sophomore." I didn't say anything, and he let himself smile slightly. "Okay, the word is that you're pretty good with pitchers. Work with your boy Phuong, especially. I want to see him throwing a decent curve by May. Halloway and Anderson will give you some hints."

"Yes, sir."

"That'll do it." He picked up his pen and went back to his paperwork. I hesitated, thinking I should try to explain Jeff to him. He looked up. "Something more?"

"Uh, just wanted to say that I'll do my best."

"Good. Because on my teams everybody does or they don't stick around very long."

"Yes, sir," I said a final time and left his office. Outside, I looked for Jeff, but he was gone. Glen, Wes, Bob Ronchetti, and a couple of the other seniors were still hanging around. I went to pack my equipment bag. "Damn, I guess somebody's got to do it," Bob muttered.

"Yeah, guess so," Wes said. Suddenly, I felt his thick arms go around my chest from behind. Bob dove for one leg, Glen for the other. Before I could get any leverage to fight back, all five of them had hold of some part of me. They lugged me to the showers and heaved me through the door. They'd plugged the drain, and I landed in four inches of freezing water, slid across the floor, and banged into the opposite wall.

"Looks more like a whale than a bull," Bob drawled.

"Welcome aboard, rook." Wes laughed. "Shut off the showers when you leave."

I splashed water at them, but they were too quick, and I heard them laughing as they slammed out the locker room door.

On my wet and very cold walk home, I started feeling a whole lot better. All my life, I'd dreamed of being a varsity ballplayer. Now I'd made it — and a year ahead of schedule. So to hell with Sandi and Billy; I had a right to feel good.

I felt an odd mix of glee and guilt about beating Jeff to the varsity. Jeff had more talent than I did. I'd always known that. But wasn't getting along with the coach part of the game? And if I could get along with Borsheim and he couldn't . . . Well, that was Jeff's problem.

By the time I reached home, I was shivering so hard that I had to take another shower to get warm. I was sitting at the foot of the stairs, pulling on fresh socks and dry shoes when Grandpa came in the back door with two bags of groceries. "More in the car?" I asked.

"No, just a quick run in and out today. Come the weekend, we'll lay in some heavy provisions. How'd practice go?"

"Pretty good. I'm second-string varsity behind Wes Halloway."

"No kidding. That's unexpected."

"Yeah. Rob Patzwald quit."

"Oh, yeah? Why?"

I couldn't hide a smile that insisted on becoming a grin. "I guess because he didn't figure he'd be ahead of me very long."

Grandpa laughed and clapped me on the shoulder. "So you made it. Well, congratulations. We'll call your mom tonight."

I shrugged. "Needn't bother. She thinks ball's a waste of time."

"No, she's gonna be proud. Don't sell her short; she's always on your side."

"Yeah, I know," I said. And the grin I couldn't hold in took over my face again.

Jeff slid into his desk in first-hour English. "Get tossed in the showers?"

"Yeah. It took them some doing, but they managed. I'd forgotten all about that ritual."

"Well, I hadn't. So, I got out of the way . . . Word is that Borsheim's gonna post final rosters third hour."

"Can't be that many cuts. By now, they'll carry just about everybody left standing."

"Yeah, but how about the sitters?"

"Knock it off, Jeff. You are not going to get cut. Just hang in there. Things will get better."

"Sure."

I took a glance at Mrs. Saxon, who had started writing furiously on the board. In about thirty seconds, she'd start laying some information on us very fast, with any laggards risking grades, egos, and pieces of their anatomy. Already, kids were scribbling in their notebooks. "Look," I said. "If for some reason you get cut, I'll quit."

He glared at me. "The hell you will. You busted your butt to make varsity, and you're going to stay there. And by the end of the season, you're gonna be ready to make everybody forget all about Wes Halloway."

Mrs. Saxon rapped her knuckles on the podium. "All right, those of you who haven't started getting the day's outline in your notebooks, get busy."

I scribbled dutifully, but when I glanced over, Jeff was frowning at his open notebook, his pen tracing a series of interlocking diamonds. Well, it didn't take Freud to figure out the symbolism there.

I got down to the gym just before lunch to check the bulletin board. The varsity roster didn't contain any surprises. Seniors held nearly all the starting spots, with a mix of seniors and juniors as backups. Phuong and I were the only sophomores. Except for Wes's big bat and the occasional pop from Bob Ronchetti in left and Mike Shields at first, we weren't going to have a lot of power. Speed looked fair, pitching pretty good — maybe even better than that if Phuong kept coming on. Still, everything figured, it was hard to imagine us finishing much higher than fourth or fifth in the league. Next year, maybe.

Billy was starting in center for Haight and the

jayvees. Love agreed with Billy, and he was playing better than he'd ever played before. Jeff was listed one from the bottom among the infielders, which meant he'd better lay in extra iodine, because he was gonna have a lot of bench splinters in his butt.

Behind me, Billy said, "All right! Starting."

I turned. "Yeah, congratulations, Billy."

"You, too, Bull." We shook. He shuffled. "Hey, Bull, I know you ain't real happy with me these days. But, you know, it just kinda happened with Sandi and me."

I nodded. "Sure, Billy. Congrats on starting. Do good." I walked off before he could finish trying to apologize. Because, frankly, I didn't give a damn. We'd been friends; now we weren't. And that meant I was done scraping Billy off the pavement. If Billy's old man turned mean again, he could beat Billy to a frigging pulp for all I cared.

Yeah, yeah, I know that wasn't fair. Mean, unkind, rude — all those things Sandi said I was. If anyone deserved a break, deserved to have somebody give a damn about him, it was Billy. But it wasn't exactly easy for me to give him that — not when it meant giving him Sandi. Because for more years than I was willing to admit, I'd figured that the day I made varsity would also be the day that Sandi finally became my girl. And from then on, she'd help me win like she'd been winning all her life — effortlessly, out of her belief that all the good things were due her, just as surely as the sun and the moon rose and set on an exact schedule to light her way.

I opened the year catching in the bull pen and pretty much stayed there. Wes got off to a great start, hitting nearly four hundred, blasting towering drives over the left-field fence, and gunning down base runners with his cannon arm. Borsheim never pulled him from a game as long as we had a chance, and that was proving more often than anybody had predicted.

With half the season to go, we were seven and three. So far, I'd caught only six innings, mopping up for Wes when we were either so far ahead or so far behind that nothing I did could make any difference. I'd gone to the plate five times, including twice as a pinch hitter, and had a single, a double, and two RBI's to show for it. Not too shabby for a sophomore scrub. Or so I told myself as I jogged out to the bull pen to spend another hour working with Phuong on his curveball while Wes got the glory.

Phuong was doing okay. Wes had coaxed him through some wild streaks in his first couple of outings, and he now had a victory to go along with a no decision and a save.

On the jayvee team, Billy was hitting line-shot singles all over the lot, stealing bases nearly every time he got on, and chasing down every fly ball within human reach. All to the wild applause of Sandi and her friends. Jeff was still on the bench, with even less to do and fewer at bats than I had. But nobody worked harder in practice or kept his mouth more grimly closed.

In the second week in May, Wes went down with a pulled hamstring in the top of the first inning of a game at Stockfarm. And from then on, my season got a lot more interesting.

I was out in the bull pen, catching Phuong's curveball, when Marc Tobin, one of the senior relievers, said, "Oh, shit. Wes is hurt."

We gathered at the fence, watching Borsheim and one of the umpires tending to Wes, where he'd taken a dive trying to leg out a slow roller down the first baseline. Frank Multerer, our number two starter, leading pessimist, and no favorite of anyone's, muttered, "It's his hamstring again. Well, there goes the damned season. Better get ready, rook. That's if your shorts are still dry."

"Hey, screw you, Frank," I said.

"Knock it off, guys," Marc said. "I think they want you, Bull."

I jogged down to the dugout as a couple of the guys helped Wes off the field. He gave me a pale smile. "Go get 'em, rook. Glen's got good stuff. Just don't get too comfortable in there. I'm playing next game."

Pete Meyer, our shortstop, struck out to end the inning, and we went on defense. Borsheim caught me by the sleeve. "Let Anderson throw what he wants. He's seen a lot of this bunch." I nodded.

I guess I should have been nervous, but crouching behind the plate, knowing that I had seven innings to catch and probably another game or two before Wes was ready again, I was suddenly exactly where I'd been born to be. I would have crowed, beaten my arms like wings, and strutted a time or two around the plate if I hadn't been afraid of appearing just a little too happy.

I had a hell of a game. Either Glen and I were on exactly the same wavelength, or Wes had conditioned him never to shake off his catcher. We got them out one right after another until the sixth, when Borsheim put in Marc to finish up. In the meantime, I doubled, scored, and added a run-scoring single to help us build a nice 5-0 lead. Then in the top of the seventh, I felt for the first time in a varsity game that sweet shiver down my bat. And despite Borsheim's warning, I hesitated at the plate for just a second to watch the ball clearing the left-field fence.

In the locker room, Borsheim came over and shook my hand. "Good job, Larsen. All the way around. Don't know what the hell we're going to do for a backup catcher until Halloway's back, but good job." He started away.

"Uh, Coach," I said. "Jeff Hanson's not getting much playing time on the jayvees. He could do it." He looked at me sharply. "Coach, he's good. He may rub people the wrong way sometimes, but he knows pitchers. He's the one who really discovered Phuong."

Borsheim tightened his lips. "Okay, I'll talk to him. But it's not going to make him a varsity ballplayer, and he's going back down the second Halloway can play."

*　*　*

I got a few of the old gang together to drill Jeff. It was the first time I'd ever seen Jeff reluctant to play ball. "I don't know, Bull," he said, flexing his legs in the shin guards. "Wearing all this stuff makes me feel like Frankenstein's monster. Maybe I ought to tell Borsheim to find somebody else."

"Oh, stop bitching and pay attention," I said.

I reviewed a few things and then we got down to business. For an hour, we worked on pitchouts and throwing to second as Dave Pickett and Billy tried to steal on him. Most of the time they got in under his throw, but he was getting better fast. He was even beginning to look like a catcher — sweat-soaked, dirty, and pissed off.

After a break, we ran through the three standard plays to stop a double steal with runners on first and third. They were tough, low percentage plays, and I could see Jeff's frustration building as Billy and Pick kept beating him. Time to call it quits.

"Okay," I yelled. "Let's do a blue, then a red, and we're done." Billy jogged back to third and Pick to first while the infielders took their positions.

Phuong's pitch smacked into Jeff's mitt, and he came out of his crouch while Ned sprinted in from short to take the decoy throw he'd fire home as Billy broke for the plate. But instead of throwing, Jeff spun and charged up the line. Billy's eyes popped. He jammed on the brakes and tried to reverse directions but lost traction, sprawling full length in the dirt as Jeff nailed him with a hard tag on the rump.

Billy scrambled up and stood glaring. Jeff came jogging back to the plate. "What the hell were you doing?" I said. "That was a red not a blue. And not much of a red, either."

"It worked, didn't it?"

"Yeah, but it wasn't the play called."

"Which wouldn't have worked, so I changed it."

I stared at him, suddenly feeling a lot like Borsheim must have felt a dozen times. "You know," I said, "Billy's been working his ass off for you, so it's just a tad horseshit to do that to him."

"I didn't do crap to him. I just changed the play, that's all."

At that point, I almost called the guys in. To hell with the arrogant little bastard. But just then Sandi rolled up on her ten-speed. Billy called, "Hey, Jim. Take my place, huh."

"Okay," I yelled. "I guess that last one was the red. Let's try the blue this time."

The play went off without a hitch, Jeff's throw going out to Ned and back to Jeff in time to catch Jim in a rundown. Jeff took off his mask and wiped his forehead. "How'd that look?"

"Pretty good," I said. "But lucky Jim was the runner. Billy would have put you on your ass after that last stunt you pulled."

101

He shrugged. "Yeah, maybe so." And Jeff surprised me, as he so often does, by doing exactly the right thing. He walked over to Billy, threw an arm over his shoulders, and gave him a hug. "Hey, thanks, Billy. Hope I didn't bruise the butt of the league's best base runner."

Billy laughed, embarrassed and pleased. Sandi said, "You be careful, Jeff. I'll have you know a certain someone's buns are this girl's personal property."

They went on kidding, and I turned away to gather up the equipment.

The following Monday, Jeff was in the bull pen with the pitchers and Jim when we played Walthrop and beat them like a drum, 14–4. I had a homer, a single, three RBI's, and gunned down two base stealers. Not a bad day's work. Jeff didn't play.

Over the next week and a half, I caught four more games and had the time of my life. Maybe it was the relief at not having to face Wes, but opposing pitchers kept throwing me fat fastballs. I showed my appreciation by knocking three home runs, three doubles, and a couple of singles. And, if Rob McHugh of Caledonia hadn't pitched a no-hitter and a two-hitter back to back, I bet I would have been conference player of the week.

Wes was still hobbling around, too sore to do anything but sit beside Borsheim and chart pitches. I felt sorry for him, because he wouldn't make all-conference if he missed much more of the season. Still, football had always been his big sport, and he'd get his athletic scholarship with or without a good baseball season.

I glanced at the wall clock and then helped myself to another pancake.

"Have you got a game this afternoon?" Grandpa asked.

"Yeah, against McArthur."

"They tough?"

"Not supposed to be. They're four–seven, I think. Where is McArthur, exactly?"

"Up on sixty-four. We drove through last fall when we took the back way up to the Willow Flowage to go fishing. Not much to the place."

"Well, their baseball team may not be so hot, but they sure got a killer girls' softball team. They're still undefeated, I think."

"The Herons? Hell, I can't remember a year they didn't take the championship. State a couple of times, too."

"Yeah, they're something. Well, I gotta run. You coming to the game?"

"I'm supposed to get my chompers checked at four, so I guess I'll miss this one. How's the schoolwork going?"

"Fine. No problems." I hesitated. "Why do you ask?"

"Your math teacher dropped off a mower the other day. Said you seemed to have a little trouble concentrating these days."

"Well, Mr. Harris is kind of a worrier."

"Not always the worst thing to be. I think if *I* lived to play baseball, I'd make sure my grades didn't upset a certain very successful career woman. And, by the way, I happen to agree with her that some things are more important than baseball."

"Like what?" I said in astonishment that was only partly jest.

He shook his head. "Well, you may be beyond hope. Still, you might try to buckle down between now and the end of the year. Just to keep your mother off my case and me off yours. *Comprende?*"

"Sure thing. See you at supper."

I thought about what he'd said while I peddled the ten blocks to school. I had to admit that since I'd made the varsity, my interest in other things had been . . . well, nonexistent. And that must have gotten pretty obvious, since usually Grandpa let me mind my business while he minded his. Okay, I'd concentrate today — not even think about the game until the last bell.

And I tried. But, God, it was tough. Class after class dragged by, while outside the sun shone on a day that Norman what's-his-name might have chosen for a painting of young men playing ball. Norman Rockwell. (See, I could still remember things if I really tried.)

Jeff and I had homerooms on the side of the building farthest from the gym, and it took us ten minutes to fight our way through the packed halls. "Did you hear Billy's getting his chance today?" he shouted.

"No. How come?"

"Ronchetti's got the flu, so Billy's starting in left."

My gut twisted for Jeff. Now Billy, who was a good ball player but no Jeff, had made it into a varsity game ahead of him. God, that must hurt. "Jeff," I said, "it's going to happen for you one of these days. Just hold on."

He waved that away. "Just worry about the game. I'm okay." He swung open the locker room door.

Phuong was at his locker three down from mine. "How you doing, ace? Ready to show these hicks how it's really done?"

Phuong gets pretty deep inside himself before a start, but he managed a smile. "I imagine I could give it a try."

"You'll be fine. Stretch good, huh?"

"Sure," he said.

As soon as I get my gear on, I always go out for a quick look at the field. Crossing the edge of the parking lot, my spikes crunching on the gravel, I gazed up, gauging the depth of the sky in case I had to handle a pop-up right above me. Could be tough — a high white haze shimmering in the heat of our first really hot day. Out in the bull pen, Jim was arranging equipment and checking the first-aid kit. I waved, and he grinned and gave me a thumbs-up. Then, at the edge of the field, I paused for a few seconds to remind myself that I was exactly where I'd always wanted to be.

Stan Olson was raking the pitcher's mound, so I went over to inspect my turf around home plate. At some parks in the conference I'd have to worry about gorges, swamps, and conspicuous ridges screwing up the game. (As in Olduvai, Great Dismal, and the foothills of the Rockies.) But at home, we have a park a lot of minor league teams would envy. Stan is the reason.

The area around the plate looked perfect, so I sauntered out to the mound. "Hey, Stan."

"How ya doing, Bull? Gonna whup 'em today?" He gave me his shy smile.

He always asks the same question before a game and, like Wes and catchers before him, I gave the same answer: "All the way to the town line."

His smile widened into a grin as he completed the good-luck formula. "And clean out of the county."

"You got it." We gave the mound a final inspection. Pitchers are supposed to check it themselves for anything that could twist an ankle. But being pitchers, they're usually too nerved up to do it. "Looks good," I said. "Appreciate it, Stan."

"Sure," he said. "Have a good game."

Borsheim came striding across the parking lot, clipboard in hand and scowl in place, while the varsity hustled to get to the field ahead of him. I joined Wes and Borsheim at the bench. "Okay," Borsheim said, consulting his clipboard. "Who do we see first?"

While Jeff warmed up Phuong and the other guys started fielding practice, we ran through McArthur's lineup. Wes reached over to tap a name. "Watch Herkert. He's the rangy kid playing catch over behind their bench. Number eight."

I found number eight among the other McArthur players and then glanced across the statistics on the clipboard. "Fair bat. What else about him?"

Wes hesitated. "Well, it's hard to explain, but the guy's a little nuts. Just when everybody's settling into a game, he'll do something weird to get people fired up. Bunt when he really shouldn't. Steal a base even though he doesn't have big-time speed. Something."

"Okay, watch him, Larsen," Borsheim said. "Anything else you can think of, Halloway?"

"Not really. They're not a bad ball club, better than four–seven, but we ought to beat them."

"Pinch hit if I need you?"

Wes grimaced. "I can swing, but I sure can't run, Coach. I mean, I'll give it a shot, but —"

Borsheim shook his head. "No. We're not going to take any chances. You've got your football scholarship to think about." He went back to studying the clipboard. "I guess we've covered it. Go ahead and bring in your boy, Larsen."

The stands were filling up as Phuong and I put the finishing touches on his warm-up. Usually, there were a lot of empty seats, but it had finally dawned on people that we actually had a shot at the conference title. A shot, that is, if we could beat Caledonia a couple of games down the line.

McArthur wasn't going anywhere in the race, but a surprising number of their fans milled about in the third-base bleachers as the team huddled up around Herkert. Behind me, McArthur's coach and Borsheim met with the home plate umpire to exchange the official lineup cards. "That'll do," I called to Phuong. I stood, stretching my back and legs.

Borsheim and McArthur's coach jogged back to their benches, and the home plate umpire turned to me. "You're new," he said.

"Yes, sir."

"Well, I'll tell you what I always told Halloway and what I'll tell McArthur's catcher. I expect catchers to be in charge on the field. Keep your boys in line, particularly your pitchers. Do not, and I mean this, *do not* complain about balls and strikes. Because I am one of your impartially short-tempered umpires: I toss anybody who gives me garbage. Got it?"

"Yes, sir." I grinned. "Phuong and I are real easy to get along with."

"Good." He turned to the field and shouted, "Play ball!"

The guys from McArthur might have been in fifth place and a far cry from being as good as the Herons, but it didn't seem anybody'd told them. We jumped out in front with three in the first, but then their pitcher got tough and didn't give us crap to hit for the next three innings. Meanwhile, with Herkert leading the show, McArthur's offense scrapped and scraped their way back to even with single runs in the second, third, and fourth. I gunned down two runners, but that didn't keep three more from stealing on me. And that pissed me off, because I wasn't used to being one down in that column.

McArthur's style rattled Phuong, and after four, he'd walked three batters, hit one, and thrown a couple of wild pitches. I calmed him down between innings, and he seemed fine when we started the top of the fifth. He got their first batter on two fastballs and a curve. Herkert came up, and Phuong threw him a fastball so mean that Herkert actually checked his bat to see if it had magically developed a baseball-sized hole. Well, try this one on, I thought, and called for a change. Herkert almost swung out of his shoes trying to catch up to what he figured would be another fastball. A second or two later, I caught Phuong's lazy change. I grinned at Herkert. "Anything you'd like to order special?"

He shrugged. "Whatever. I ain't fussy."

It was a good comeback, but I knew that we had him so confused now that he'd miss just about anything Phuong threw. I called a curve and set up low on the inside half. Phuong went into his windup, coming over the top to drop it right at Herkert's knees. And with two strikes on him, the goofy bastard squared and laid a perfect bunt down the third baseline. Carl Hanes, who was playing well back at third, never had a chance, and Herkert legged it out easily. The McArthur fans did some whooping as Herkert pumped his fist in the air a couple of times. I stood behind the plate, glaring at him, but he didn't look my way. Okay, I thought, just don't get too comfortable out there.

I crouched as their next batter stepped into the box. I gave Phuong the sign to come in with a heater straight down the pipe. By this time I knew Mike Shields, our first baseman, pretty well, and I planned to fire a pickoff behind Herkert to see if I could get him leaning the wrong way. Good plan, except that Phuong threw the heater high and about a yard inside. The batter bailed out with a yelp, and I barely got my mitt up in time to knock it down to hold Herkert at first.

"Did you call that?" the umpire snapped at me.

"No, sir. That one just got away from him."

"Uh, Mr. Umpire, sir," the batter said. We looked at him. "That pitch hit me. Just brushed my shirt."

"The hell," I started to say, but swallowed it.

"Take your base," the umpire said, and glared at me. The McArthur fans cheered as Herkert pumped his fist in the air and trotted down to second.

I jogged out to the mound to have a word with Phuong. "Just like old times," he muttered.

"Nah," I said. "We're beyond all that. We got the first guy easy, now let's get this one. Then we'll be almost out of it."

He took a breath. "Give it a try, I guess."

"Right. Now I don't know if Herkert's smart enough to steal a sign, but we won't take any chances. So fastball, fastball, waste a cutter, then finish him off with another fastball. Got it?"

"Yeah, I got it."

But he didn't. The two fastballs missed the outside corner by a foot, the cutter bounced, and the last fastball seemed to give up as it sailed high and wide for ball four. The batter jogged down to first, and Borsheim came out of the dugout, already signaling to the bull pen.

I joined him at the mound. "Don't worry, Tiger," he said to Phuong. "We'll get you out of it." Phuong nodded and slouched off toward the bench as Marc Tobin came running in. "You warm?" Borsheim asked him.

"Yes, sir."

"Good. Okay, let your defense play ball. If we get down by a run, we'll get it back in our half. What I don't want is a lot of cutting it too fine and walking guys. Okay?" We nodded.

I crouched to take Marc's warm-ups. Marc has decent stuff, great control, and the nerves of a high-wire artist. Still, I was worried about Brenner, McArthur's big first baseman, who'd almost reached the fence on us in the first and had hit a long drive just foul in the third. And it was while I was thinking hard how to handle him that I forgot one tiny little detail that was about to change the game, my season, and maybe my life. "That's five," the umpire called. "Play ball."

Brenner took Marc's first pitch for a strike, let a ball

111

go by, and then fouled the next one into the stands behind us. Okay, now we've got you, I thought. I called a fastball low on the inside corner. Brenner was a pretty good hitter, but nobody handles that pitch very well if it comes in right where it's supposed to. And that's where Marc put it. Brenner swung, scalping the ball and sending it spinning and hissing out in front of the plate. I lunged for it, snared it inches from going foul, and spun to look Herkert back to third before throwing to first.

And the goofy bastard was coming home! I couldn't believe it. Nobody, not even somebody as fast and ballsy as Jeff, would risk coming home on a squibber in front of the plate. Not with a base open. I charged him before he had time to turn back. *Happy to oblige you, you silly son of a —*

We met a dozen feet from the plate, up close and real personal. And, yeah, I tagged him hard. Tagged him hard, because he needed to know that I didn't take kindly to hicks from up north leading cheers in my ballpark. Not in front of my fans and the girl who was going to be my girl once she got over whatever stupid fantasy she'd built up around Billy. Here you played by the Bull's rules. But, so help me God, I never meant to tag him in the face.

I aimed the tag at his shoulder, but when he ducked his head trying to get around me, I missed and nailed him square in the nose. I think I felt the crunch, but my brain didn't record the significance until later. His

112

shoulder slammed into my chest, and I went down, but I was rolling before I hit, bouncing to my feet, ready to gun down any other McArthur runner stupid enough to try to steal a base on me.

I was greeted by a stunned silence, then loud boos from the McArthur fans. Nobody was running on the bases, and suddenly things seemed out of kilter. What the hell was going on? I looked at Marc, who stood a few feet away, his mouth open. "My God, Bull," he said. "The bases were loaded. You had a force at home."

"But second —" I stammered.

"The kid who got hit was on second."

And I remembered the batter after Herkert — the kid who might or might not have been brushed by the wild Phuong-ball. How the hell had I forgotten him?

I looked at Herkert in horror. He lay curled up, both hands over his face, blood squirting through his fingers. The umpire knelt next to him, a hand on his shoulder, as McArthur's coach and another adult pushed by me with a big first-aid kit. The umpire stood then, a ferocious tower of a man. He pointed to both benches. "Everybody sit down! There's going to be no brawling here." He turned on me. God, I hadn't felt so small since grade school. "You meathead!" he snarled. "Get off my field."

"But —" I started.

"You're out of here!" he bellowed.

At my elbow, I heard Marc hiss, "For God's sake,

Bull, get out of here before you make everything worse."

I went, passing Borsheim, who was marching grim-faced to the scene of the disaster. I waited long enough to see them get Herkert to his feet, off the field, and into a car for the trip to the emergency room. Then I crossed the edge of the parking lot, my chin about as low as it could go, to the showers.

I must have been in shock, because it didn't occur to me that Jeff would have to catch the rest of the game. Despite everything, I wish I could have seen him in his first varsity game. The guys said he did okay, catching or blocking everything through the last two innings. He came up for the first time with two outs in the bottom of the seventh, slicing a single to right to keep us briefly in the game before McArthur recorded the last out and went home with a 4–3 victory. That they had that fourth run at all was, of course, my fault. The umpire had in-voked the unsportsmanlike-conduct rule and given Herkert the score that I could have stopped by stepping on home plate. And I felt like crap.

Borsheim came in while the guys were showering and waved me into his office. "We just got word that Herkert's going to be okay. Broken nose, but he's got a hard head so they don't figure any concussion." I nod-ded, looking at my shoes. "But you got that umpire mightily upset, and he was going to recommend a three-game suspension."

I stared at him. "Three —"

He held up a palm. "I talked him down to two. Had to kiss his ass to do it, but he agreed. That's the best you're gonna get. And don't start thinking about appeals like you were some kind of big leaguer. This is high school ball, and I've never heard of the league overruling an official. So you've got a vacation. Spend it thinking hard."

"Can I travel with the team?"

He shook his head. "Nope. You can practice, and you can sit in the stands in your street clothes, that's all. But, look, that boy's going to be okay. Let's at least be thankful for that." He shoved things around on his desk, and then picked up the phone.

I had my hand on the doorknob, when he said, "And, Bull, don't think you're the first ballplayer who ever screwed up. It happens." It wasn't until later that I realized he'd used my nickname for the first time.

Jeff was waiting for me at the locker room door. "If I were you, I'm not sure I'd walk with me," I said.

"Don't be stupid," he said. "Besides, there might be some McArthur fans waiting around the corner with tire irons, and I wouldn't want to miss seeing you rough 'em up. . . . So, what'd Borsheim say?"

"Herkert's going to be okay. The umpire's telling the league to suspend me for two games."

"Ouch. Double ouch, come to think of it. Means I'll have to catch."

"Don't gloat."

"Believe me, I'm not. I got through today, but this catching stuff scares the hell out of me."

"I'll bet," I said.

Ahead, Phuong, Jim, Billy, and Sandi sat on a picnic table. When Sandi saw us, she gave Billy a quick kiss and hopped on her ten-speed. "Some friends of yours," Jeff said.

"Two of 'em, anyway."

He glanced at me. "Three," he said. "And don't you forget it. Whether you want to count Sandi as another is up to you."

I gave Grandpa the story in all its gory detail. "So, that boy's going to be okay?" he asked.

"That's what Coach heard."

"Well, let's hope so. . . . " He sipped his coffee. "Pardon me for saying this, but don't you think you should be feeling just a bit sorrier?"

I lifted my hands and let them fall. "If he just hadn't been running so darned hard . . . I mean, he was going to be out by a mile."

"So? Wasn't there a chance you'd drop the ball or miss the plate?"

I shrugged. "A chance, I guess."

"What you're really saying is that he shouldn't have been playing hard. But I've never seen you or Jeff dog it."

I wanted to protest, wanted to explain why Herkert

116

deserved a good crunch short of the plate for trying to show me up. But then I thought of him curled up on the ground, his hands covering his face, and his blood soaking into the dirt. I looked down at my hands, lying big and strong and helpless on the worn tabletop.

Grandpa sighed and reached over to give my shoulder a squeeze. "I don't want to seem hard on you, Grandson. I know you feel like hell about losing that game, but take it from one who knows, there's no good in bullshitting yourself. It just makes everything worse." He got up to start making supper.

The team played Wednesday at Sullivan Mills, a little town twenty miles south of Shipley. Jeff played well, getting two singles and allowing only a single passed ball. But with Wes, Bob Ronchetti (who still wasn't over the flu), and me out of the lineup, there wasn't a lot of power left. The Mills won 3–2, dropping us into third, three back of Caledonia.

I was disconsolately sweeping the floor of the garage late Friday afternoon when Grandpa sighed, put down the saw blade he was sharpening, and stared at me. "Are you sick or just feeling sorry for yourself?" he asked.

I shrugged. "Just wish I was going over to Caledonia with the team tomorrow. Big game."

"You could drive over there and watch."

"You'd let me drive that far by myself?"

117

"Might as well knock the sheen off that new license of yours sometime."

I thought it over for a moment. "No, I couldn't watch from the stands. It'd hurt too much."

"Well, Monica and I are goin' fishing. You could come along with us."

Go fishing with Grandpa and Monica McGivern, my former third-grade teacher? Not a chance. "No, thanks. I'll just stick around here."

"Suit yourself. But if I were you, I'd do something to get my mind off things."

"Got any suggestions?"

"Well, you could drive up to McArthur and tell that boy you're sorry."

"Andy Herkert? I couldn't do that."

"Doesn't he have it coming?"

I nodded glumly. "Yeah, I guess."

"So why not go tell him?"

"Probably hit me with a bat."

"Oh, I don't think so. I called his mom and dad a couple of nights ago. They sounded like pretty nice folks."

Of course, he would. "How's Andy doing?" I asked.

"Good. No permanent damage. No hard feelings, either. Or not so far as I could tell."

I considered, tempted by the prospect of a long drive alone. "No, I couldn't face him. I'll send him a card."

Grandpa shrugged. "Next best thing, I guess." He picked up the saw blade again.

* * *

I rolled over a little after six the next morning and squinted at the day. The robins were making a ruckus in the mountain ash outside my window as sunlight streamed through the branches to flood my room with spring. Whatever my mind argued, my body told me it was time to be up and doing. But doing what?

Grandpa was packing the old station wagon he calls his fishing car. "You feeling okay?" he asked. "I haven't seen you up this early on a Saturday since you hit puberty."

"I'm okay."

"Want to go fishing?"

"No, thanks. Thought maybe I'd drive to McArthur, after all. Or at least head up that way."

"Got money for gas?"

"Yeah, I've got some."

"Well, drive careful. Give my regards to the Herkerts. You going to cut the grass before you go or leave it until tomorrow?"

Long grass is one of the few sore points between Grandpa and me. "I'll cut it this morning."

"Good boy."

I had to wait for the dew to dry before I could cut the grass, so it was late morning before I actually got on the road. I drove northeast from Shipley in bright sunshine, the rolling farmland giving way gradually to forest and lakes.

At a convenience store just past the sign announcing

"McArthur, unincorporated," I filled the gas tank for a quick getaway and got directions to Andy's house. I drove to the far edge of town, half expecting a wreck of a place with rusting cars in the front yard and snapping bearhounds out back. But it was a freshly painted white farmhouse with a couple of outbuildings and a well-tended lawn.

A husky, dark-haired girl about my age was bagging the leaves she'd raked from under the bushes beneath the bay window. Not quite believing I was actually doing it, I got out of the car and walked across the lawn. "Hi," she said. "Can I help you?"

"Uh, yeah. I'm Neil Larsen from Shipley. Is Andy around?"

"Hey, you're the Bull, aren't you? I heard about you big time." She laughed, showing strong, white teeth.

"Uh, yeah," I said. "I'm the Bull."

"I'm Bev, Andy's little sister. Chronologically, that is. Andy just went to the store. He'll be home in a few minutes. Want some lemonade?"

"Uh, sure. That'd be good."

She led me inside, told me to sit at the kitchen table, and brought over a jar of cookies and a pitcher of lemonade. "Don't worry. Nothing's poisoned. We're not mad at you or anything."

"Not even Andy?"

"Well, I guess his nose is a little bent out of shape." She laughed.

"So to speak," I said.

"And more. But relax. My parents only learned how to quit having kids a few years ago, and there are eight of us playing sports. Heck, somebody's always in a cast or on crutches. We play hard, and we get banged up a lot. I even took a first-aid course at the vocational school last winter so I could bandage my brothers and sisters."

"Do any work on Andy's nose?"

"A little. I think he's kind of proud of his broken schnoz."

"Good," I said. "Or I guess that's good."

"Let's just call it okay. Can't go to extremes. Bring a glove?"

"No. I didn't think I'd need one."

"Around here you will. Come on, I'll lend you one of Andy's."

We played catch on the front lawn. She threw hard, not shot-putting it like most girls, but free and easy in a smooth three-quarter motion. "You throw pretty good," I said.

"For a girl." She laughed, and pegged one sidearm. Nice.

She brought the next one in overhand, then, laughing, dropped down and submarined one at me. "Wow," I said. "You want a job? We could use you in Shipley."

"Not a chance. I'm McArthur true and blue. We've got a mean girls' softball team up here."

"The Herons? Sure, I've seen you written up in the sports pages. What do you play?"

"Third, mostly, but I've done a little pitching. Let me get a softball, and I'll show you my stuff."

I crouched and let her burn in a few. She was good. "Take something off," I called. "I want to see your change."

She frowned. "I don't have much of one. I tip it with my motion."

"Give it a shot. We'll figure it out."

"Okay. I never shake off my catcher."

"Good principle."

She started working on the change, and after a dozen throws and a couple of suggestions, started getting it disguised. We were concentrating so hard that we didn't hear the car until the door slammed. I stood, recognizing Andy Herkert — which wasn't too tough seeing that he had a huge bandage over his nose. "Hi, Andy," I said. "Neil Larsen from Shipley."

He hesitated and then came forward, his hand outstretched. "Yeah, we sorta met, didn't we?" We shook. He shuffled, more embarrassed than I was.

"How's the nose?" I asked.

He shrugged. "Okay. Wakes me up when I roll over on it in the night, but it's getting better."

"I'm sorry, Andy. I just went stupid for a second and forgot about the force-out at home."

"That's okay. It was a tight game and things happen.

122

I appreciate you coming to see me." He hesitated. "Heard you got suspended for a couple of games."

I nodded. "Yeah, they're playing Caledonia without me today." '

"What a bunch of crap. A guy can make a mistake. They don't have to make a big deal out of it."

That was a hell of a lot more generous than I would have been. "Uh, when's the doctor going to let you play?"

"More like when's my mom going to let me play. Maybe Monday. We've got a make-up game scheduled against Sullivan Mills."

"We played them the other night. The guys did, that is. Lost three–two."

"I read that. How far does that put you behind Caledonia?"

"Three games."

"Ouch. Tough to catch them now."

"Yeah, real tough."

"Hey," Bev called. "If you guys are going to gab all day, at least do it while you're playing catch." She tossed Andy a glove.

We got in a triangle and started tossing the ball around. Andy tried to trick Bev by flipping one behind his back, but she caught it and whipped it on to me without so much as a hitch in her motion. Andy shook his head. "Darned girls are a bunch of show-offs in this town. . . . Say, that pitcher of yours with the funny name is something else. What kind of name is that, anyway?"

"Vietnamese."

"I figured something like that. A few of us went to scout him when you guys played in Mosinee a couple of weeks ago. He was sure on that night. Zap, zap, zap. Inside corner, outside corner. Up, down, and nothing downtown. How many strikeouts did he have, anyway?"

"Nine or ten, I think."

"Well, we talked all the way back how he'd kill us if we didn't shake him up early. And that's how we came to play."

"It worked."

"Well, he's only a sophomore, and no offense, but I ain't seen a sophomore yet who doesn't get a little shook when you start playing games with his head."

"Andy's good at the psychology," Bev said. "Might not be able to define it or spell it, but he knows how to use it."

"Yeah," I said. "I learned."

He shrugged. "Hey, it's part of the game."

I glanced at my watch. "I'd better get on the road pretty soon."

"Nah," Bev said. "We've just gotten started. Stay for supper. Afterward, we'll play some real ball."

"Sure," Andy said. "That's one thing about this family; you can always get up a game."

I started to make an excuse, but Bev cut me off.

"You'll insult Ma if you don't stay. You can bust her kid's nose but don't turn down her cooking."

The rest of the family started coming home, and before I knew it, I was wedged into a space at the supper table, passing huge platters of food. Andy and I got a lot of ribbing about our collision, and I heard about a dozen stories of other Herkert injuries. As Bev said, they played hard and had the scars and broken bones to prove it.

After supper, the whole family and half a dozen neighbor kids played softball. I played right, aware as always that God had passed me by when he'd handed out the speed. Bev played center, covering her territory and a good deal of mine.

A couple innings into the game, after I'd had the satisfaction of parking one down the line in left, Andy hit a high fly to the right center-field alley. I was going all out to get under it when I heard Bev coming hard from center. I tried to dive out of the way. Too late: the ball smacked into her glove a second before she plowed into me, and we went down in a heap. She lay on top of me, laughing and gasping for breath, then pushed herself up on her hands and grinned down at me. A couple of her blouse buttons had come undone, and I could see beads of sweat shining between her breasts. "You don't seem so tough," she said. "Heck, if it'd been me trying to score on that squibber, I would have run you right over." She rolled off, hopped to her feet, and threw the ball back to the infield.

We played until dark. Her mom said that it was too

late for me to drive back, so I called Grandpa. "It's going okay, then?" he asked.

"Oh, yeah, we're having a good time."

"Good. Well, stay out of trouble. I'll see you tomorrow."

When I got off the phone, Bev said, "Come on. Let's walk down to the Dairy Queen. I'll buy."

"That's okay. I've got money."

I started to look around for Andy, but she looped an arm through mine and whispered, "Come on. He's calling his girl, and she'll keep him on the phone for an hour."

We took the long way home from the Dairy Queen, hand in hand. It seemed natural somehow, and on a dark section of the street, she swung around to face me and it seemed natural to kiss her, too. Out behind the toolshed, where the sky opened up with a trillion stars, we did that and a little bit more, until she pushed me away and grinned. "We go any further, and you're going to get a bad impression of McArthur girls."

"Not really."

"Then you'll get a bad impression of this one. Come on, I'll show you where Mom wants you to bed down."

And that was it. In the morning, as they were getting ready for church, I thanked everyone. Bev said I could stick around for Sunday dinner, but I said I'd better get going.

"Don't be a stranger," she said. "The Dairy Queen is open all summer." She nudged me and winked.

* * *

"And suppose they hadn't been such nice people? Suppose there'd been a lawsuit?"

I shifted the phone to my other ear and tried to sound reasonable. "Mom, it was an accident in a game. Nobody sues about them."

"Ha! Out here, everybody sues about everything."

"Well, I guess we're just behind the times in the boonies."

"Don't be sarcastic with me, young man!"

"I wasn't, Mom. I'm just trying to explain that it was no big deal. Grandpa shouldn't have worried you with it."

"You'd prefer that he kept things from your mother?"

"No, Mom."

"He told me you were suspended. That's not a big deal?"

There was a long pause. Finally, I said, "I'm sorry, Mom. I learned a lesson."

She made an irritable sound that signified impatience, frustration, and a dozen or so other motherly emotions. "Well, I'm beginning to think it's time for you to come out here. Have a look at the wider world. I know some places where you could get a summer job. Or we could look into a summer school program."

I groaned. "Mom, I don't want to spend my summer in Los Angeles. Too hot, too many weird people."

"If you stay there, you're certainly not going to spend *all* summer playing baseball."

127

"I never do. I help Grandpa, and I cut half the lawns in the neighborhood. And I do some reading. I'm not a complete mental slug."

She grumbled a bit and then said, "Well, let me talk to your grandfather."

Grandpa took over again and spent a few minutes listening and saying "Yes, honey" before finally hanging up the phone.

I snapped at him. "Why'd you tell her? She didn't have to know."

He looked at me mildly. "She was going to find out anyway. She takes the local fish wrapper, remember?"

"Yeah, but she doesn't read the sports pages."

"Sure, she does. She's not going to miss the chance to see her kid's name in print."

"Well, the paper didn't make a big deal —"

He held up a palm. "Neil, she's your mother. And that gives her the right to know what's going on with you."

"Then how come she didn't stick around here and act like it?"

He raised his eyebrows. "I haven't heard you say that in a long while. Really mean it?"

I looked down, surprised at the pain that I thought I'd put behind me a long time ago. "No, I guess not."

"You can always go to LA."

I didn't look at him. "Do you want me to go?"

"No, of course not. You'll be gone too soon the way it is. Two years probably sounds like a long time to you,

128

but believe me, it hardly seems like anything when you're my age. Now cheer up. Let's go get some ice cream."

Monday morning, the guys were still shaking their heads about the game in Caledonia. Glen had given up six runs in an inning and two-thirds, and no one out of our bull pen could slow them down, either. Meanwhile, Rob McHugh gave up a total of four hits — an average game for him. Final score, 14–0.

"How'd you do?" I asked Jeff.

He snorted. "How could anyone do against that bunch? They're so damned good they've got Joe Spence sitting the bench and Hank Lutz doing set up work out of the bull pen."

"Get a hit?"

"Yeah, I beat out a slow roller, but it didn't end up counting for anything."

"How'd the catching go?"

"I didn't exactly shine, but I didn't make a fool out of myself, either. Melcher stole a couple on me, but they were hitting the ball so often nobody else bothered to try. We were bush, and they knew it."

"Maybe next time."

"Yeah, maybe. But it's a plenty big maybe."

My suspension was over, but we didn't have another game until Wednesday and by that time Wes was ready to play. I went back to the bull pen, where I sat with Jim and Jeff, watching the team win without us. At least Borsheim had decided that Jeff could stay with the varsity, and that was something.

The team won again on Saturday. I had a pinch double in the fifth. Jeff went in to run for me and stayed to play the last two innings at short. The victory put us at eleven and six, and we could finish third by winning two of our last three games. But that wasn't going to be easy against Caledonia, McArthur, and Sullivan Mills, who'd all beaten us once already.

Caledonia came to town first, and I had a chance to see what all the head shaking had been about. Even with most of their seniors sitting out the last few innings, they were some machine. Final score: Caledonia 9, Shipley 1. But our one run was mine on a long drive to left center — a shot that let them know that there would be another season.

Two days later, we bussed up to McArthur. Andy Herkert and the boys tried their old tricks, but Wes calmed them down by picking one guy off first and gunning down two more at second. Meanwhile, Frank Multerer kept the ball down and, except for a golf shot by Brenner over the right-field fence, kept them from scoring.

We won 7–1, an easy victory that only reminded me how I'd been to blame for the loss the first time we'd played. Borsheim kept me out of the game, which was probably a good idea. Climbing on the bus for the ride back to Shipley, I saw the Herons' bus pulling into the parking lot. I hesitated on the step. Behind me, Jeff said, "Forget something?"

"No, I guess not," I said.

Sandi caught me at my locker on the Friday before finals week. "Bull, can we talk?"

"Sure. Seem to be talking now."

"No, I mean really talk."

"Okay. Let's sit together at lunch."

"No, I'm skipping lunch so I fit into my new jeans. Let's go for a walk."

Did it occur to her that I might want to eat lunch? No. Did it occur to me to say so? No. But what else was new?

We strolled across the parking lot toward the ball field. Stan Olson's new pickup was parked on the edge of the field, and we could see Stan on his tractor, cutting the grass in center field. "Last game of the season, tomorrow," I said. "Want to go out afterward and celebrate?"

She took my arm. "You know I love you, Bull, but no thanks. Billy and I have some real important stuff to do."

"I'll bet."

"Really. I've been making him study every night this week, and we're going to study tomorrow night, too. Even if it is a Saturday."

"Good for you."

"He's really trying, Bull. But it's hard for him. He's smart, but it's like he's got too much else on his mind to

131

concentrate on schoolwork. You know, problems at home. His dad's started getting mean again, and . . ."

I didn't want to hear this. I was done with Billy and his problems. I stopped in my tracks. "What do you want me to do, Sandi? I've been through this crap with Billy for years. And last summer, we finally got him some help. Billy's got a lot of people he can turn to. So what exactly do you want from me?"

"He won't ask them. None of them." She bit her lower lip, tears filling her eyes.

I took a deep breath and stared upward at the high blue of the sky. God, I didn't need this. "Why don't you talk to Jeff?"

"Jeff hates me. He's always hated me."

"No, Sandi, he doesn't hate you. He just doesn't have the illusions some of us have about you."

"What's that supposed to mean?"

"Never mind." I stared at her, wondering why I still loved her when I liked Gwen Schmidt, Bev Herkert, and about a dozen other girls ten times more. "Look," I said, "I really don't want to get involved. I'll talk to Jeff, but that's it, Sandi. That's more than I owe and all I'm going to give."

She wiped her eyes, and said in that little-girl voice that I'd heard just a few times too many in the last ten years, "Thanks, Bull. You do know I love you."

"Sure," I said. "Just all to pieces."

*   *   *

Jeff nodded glumly. "Yeah, I thought the signs were all there. What are we going to do?"

"No, Jeff. It's what are you going to do."

"You're walking out on it?"

"I'm walking."

He sighed. "Look, Bull. You, me, Jim, and Billy go back a long —"

I stood and walked out. Screw 'em.

The stands were about two-thirds full for our last game of the season. Sullivan Mills was in, and we whupped on them like we should have the first time. Glen was sharp as a razor, his big roundhouse curve nearly jerking shoulders out of joint. Wes and Bob Ronchetti both hit home runs with men aboard, and we were ahead 7–1 when Borsheim started pulling the seniors in ones and twos so that they could get a hand from the crowd. He gave Wes the honor of coming out first. I met him with a handshake at the on-deck circle. "It's all yours, rook," he said. "Don't screw it up." And I couldn't answer for the lump in my throat that didn't go away until I caught Glen's first roundhouse swooping in across the plate.

In the next inning, Billy took Ronchetti's place in left and Jeff went in for Pete Meyer at short. Glen turned things over to Marc Tobin. After being humiliated by Glen, the guys from Sullivan Mills beat the crap out of Marc, which was too bad since he was a nice guy and deserved better in his last outing as a senior. With two runs in, runners on first and third, and still nobody out, Borsheim pulled Marc.

While Phuong jogged in to take the load, Borsheim rubbed up the ball in his big hands. "Let the Tiger get us out of this jam, and then we'll let the last seniors in the pen finish up."

I stared at him. The seniors in the pen meant Jerry Addison and Matt Ronchetti, Bob's cousin. Neither of them had much for stuff and had been used almost exclusively as batting practice pitchers. Borsheim returned my look evenly. "You'll understand someday, son. But right now, getting those two seniors in means as much to me as winning this game."

I took Phuong's warm-up pitches and then we got to work on the next batter. I kept an eye on the runner at first. If he got a lousy jump, I'd try to get him going into second. Otherwise, I'd let him have it free rather than taking a chance with the runner on third. But to my surprise, he never tried for second, and we got the batter on two fastballs and a sucker curve.

The next batter hesitated in the on-deck circle, reading the coach's signs. I glanced quickly at first and third, trying to pick up something from how the runners were following the signs. Then I knew, without knowing quite how, that they'd move on the first pitch.

I waited while the batter got comfortable in the box, then stood and shouted, "Blue!" I crouched quickly, and before the batter could think to step out, Phuong came in with a fastball. The runner on first broke, and I was up, firing the ball not at second but at a spot behind the mound. Jeff charged, caught the ball thigh high, and fired it back home. I caught it and spun, ready to go down on one knee to matador the runner trying to slide by me to the plate. But he slammed on the brakes, his eyes like saucers, and tried to turn back. He was way, way too late, and slow as I was, I caught him in half a dozen steps.

I was still shaking my head when I got back to the plate. "God, was that dumb," I said to the batter. "He didn't have a prayer of getting back to third."

The kid shrugged. "Tom's kind of vain about his nose. Didn't want you rearranging it for him."

"You guys heard about that, huh?"

He snorted. "Hell, who hasn't? You got a rep, friend." He kicked a hole for his back foot and reset himself. "So is this kid going to give me anything to hit?"

"Nah. But get ready to duck. He doesn't like people digging in on him."

"Thanks for telling me now."

Phuong put him away with three fastballs. We got a run back in the bottom of the inning. Then two innings of surprisingly good work by Jerry Addison and Matt Ronchetti and we had a win and third place.

Borsheim stood in the middle of the locker room. "This is a good team. Next year it's going to be a better team. And every one of you graduating seniors will be able to take pride in that, because you helped the younger players learn to play winning ball. So we expect to hear from you, and we expect to see you at the games whenever you can make it. Best of luck to you all." There was a smattering of applause. Most of the seniors and quite a few of the rest of us seemed to be having trouble not crying. Because, win or lose, it had been good to be together.

When I looked at Borsheim again, his lips were set a little too tight and his eyes were moist. God, the guy had a heart; it was hard to believe. "Hanson, come in here a minute," he said gruffly, and led the way to his office.

We had a couple of hours before everybody was getting together for pizza. Jeff and I walked over to his house. "What'd Borsheim want?" I asked.

"Nothing much. Just told me that if I didn't screw up, I'd be starting shortstop next year."

"Hey, congratulations. 'Bout time he saw the light."

"Thanks. Uh, there's one more thing. He said he's making me team captain."

I stared at him. "You're kidding me. After all the crap between you two this year?"

He shrugged. "Hey, the dude's got a different way of doing things, but I think he knows how to win."

"Sort of like you."

"Maybe . . . You pissed?"

"You know better than that. I may kill you to get the job, but I'm not exactly pissed."

"Good. Because I wouldn't even be on the varsity if you hadn't hung by me."

"Let's get off this sloppy shit. What do you want to do tomorrow?"

"The usual, I guess. How about you?"

"The same."

"After all, you know what they say: On the seventh day —"

"God made baseball. Yeah, you said that before."

And laughing, we climbed the hill toward the park, where General McPherson stood waiting patiently through the seasons.

FALL – JUNIOR YEAR

"How I Spent My Summer Vacation"

1. My mom made me go to Los Angeles and kept me there for six excruciating weeks.
2. I returned a forgotten man.
3. I got dumped on by my best friend.
4. I played some ball.
5. My grandpa got a new lady friend and took no notice of me.
6. My sort-of girlfriend ignored me.
7. I lost most of my lawn-mowing jobs and became impoverished.
8. I went to work for Parks and Recreation.
9. I returned to school.
10. I got this stupid assignment.

If you insist on more detail, let's at least try to make it quick. I should have taken Mom seriously when she started talking about bringing me to LA for "a look at the wider world." Two days before the end of school, my plane ticket and orders arrived. I *would* come to LA, I *would* interview for the job she'd found for me, and I *would* enjoy the experience. No discussion scheduled, no argument allowed.

At that point, I wasn't too worried. I figured that after a week living with a teenager, she'd be more than happy to send me home. Then Jeff and I would get serious about training a team for summer league.

Wrong again, Big Fella. Mom didn't budge from her plan. The morning after I arrived, she had me interviewing for a job as a "mail-delivery technician" with the big insurance company across the street from her office. And despite my efforts to seem unenthusiastic during the interview, I got the job. The next day, wearing white shirt, tie, and dark slacks, I began pushing the mail cart through the halls. A zombie could have done the job, but Mom saw it as my first real work experience. I pointed out that I'd been mowing lawns since I was eleven and helping Grandpa even longer, but she dismissed that as: "odd jobs in a small place; this is real work in a real city."

Then how come I was already sensing significant atrophy of my brain functions? Could this be good? Could this be proper conditioning for work in corporate

America? Apparently so, since she didn't bother to respond to my questions.

Living in LA was a bore. If you can't believe that, try it at sixteen with no girl, no car, no money, and a paranoid mother. While she schmoozed clients until ten or eleven every night, I sat around her apartment under strict orders not to set foot outside. Some wider world.

By the third week, confinement and fluorescent lighting had just about driven me nuts. I called Grandpa. (Again.) He sighed. "So, you really can't hack it there, huh?"

"I can hack it, Grandpa, but I don't want to hack it. And why should I? I can make just as much money mowing lawns back home; I won't be in Mom's way; and I'll have more fun."

"I doubt if your mother thinks of you as being in the way."

"Well, probably not, since I hardly see her. Come on, Grandpa. Will you talk to her?"

There was a long pause. "I'm not sure I can do that anymore, Neil. If anything's got to be said, I think you're going to have to do the saying."

"But, Grandpa, don't you want me home —"

"Neil, don't start that. Your grandmother and I got you over that being-wanted business a long time ago. Of course I want you here. But we've known all along that this would happen someday. Your mother may not show it very well sometimes, but she loves you. And

141

because she's ambitious, that love comes across as big ambitions for you."

"I'm a mail boy, Grandpa. Baboons could do this work."

"They can probably mow lawns, too."

"But I'm going to make my living playing ball. Or at least that's how I'm going to pay for college. Which means I should be home playing in summer league."

He sighed again. "I know what your ambitions are, Neil. I'm not convinced that they're very practical, but they're yours and you've got a right to them. But you're the one who's going to have to convince your mother."

"Grandpa, I already told you that she won't listen to me."

He hesitated. "All right, I'll try to talk her into letting you come back for a few weeks. But, Grandson, I wouldn't count on staying here. Come the fall, I think she's going to have other plans for you."

"Come again?"

"A school in California. Maybe a boarding school. Maybe a private school where you'd come home nights. She called me the other day to ask if I'd mind. She also sent me some brochures, and frankly, some of those places look pretty impressive."

When I finally got my breath back, I managed, "What'd you tell her?"

"I said I'd miss you, but that she was the boss."

"And that's all?"

"What else could I say? I would, but she is."

I stared at the phone for a long minute, then mumbled, "Good night, Grandpa." I think he tried to say something, but I hung up.

I went for a long walk, covering block after block of the night streets Mom had forbidden me to walk. I half hoped somebody would hassle me, because I was big and angry and very ready to take out my loneliness on the world.

Two hours later, I found myself near the apartment again. I stepped into a newsstand and bought a package of thick, black cigars. Upstairs, I lit one, nearly fainted when I tried to inhale, and then set it on a saucer to smoke by itself. I puffed on it now and then to keep it going, and when it was done, I lit a second.

I was burning a third when Mom came in. She stared at me in horror. "What on earth are you doing?"

"Smoking a cigar. I do it all the time at home. Grandpa doesn't mind."

"Put it out this instant!" She marched to a window and threw it open. "I don't know what point you think you're making, young man. But . . ."

I let her rail. I'd promised myself to be calm — oh, the very soul of reasonableness. But I didn't put out the cigar. Finally, I blew out a cloud of blue smoke and said, "The point is, Mom, that you can't make me do anything I don't want to. I go along with a lot of stuff because you're my mother. But you can't actually *make* me do anything." She stood, hands on hips, glaring at me. "And before you start insisting that you can, let me give you a couple of examples. First, I don't like this job, and if I decide to quit tomorrow, there's not going to be a damned thing you can do about it."

"Don't swear."

"Not one *damned* thing. And a second little issue is where I live. I am not coming out here to go to school. I'm staying in Shipley, no matter what you say."

"I am your mother and your legal guardian. And that means I can make you go to school anywhere I want."

"Oh, sure," I agreed. "We can go into the legal system. Police, the courts, social workers. I'm sure you've got lots of time for that. And, meanwhile, I'll be hopping a bus or hitchhiking home every time you turn your back."

"I'll put you in a boarding school."

"Well, it better have high walls, strong locks, and real big guards, because I am going to be hell to keep there."

"Now you just see here—"

I smashed my fist on the table. "You see here! You have been gone from my life most of the last sixteen years, and it's just a little damned late to start trying to take over now."

"And I imagine you think if I'd given you a father—"

"I don't imagine anything! I was just fine with Grandma and Grandpa. If you decided to bury the guy in a swamp, that was your decision."

She stared at me. "Buried him in a swamp?"

I waved a hand. "Just a figure of speech."

She sat down on the couch, still staring at me. Then

she did the thing I least expected; she began laughing, looking suddenly girlish. "Well, I'll admit that doing that and worse to him crossed my mind once upon a time. But tell me true, do you blame me for not marrying him? Believe me, he wasn't worth it."

"Mom, that was your business. I don't blame you."

She studied me for a long minute. "You know, you can't stay in Shipley forever," she said quietly.

"Grandpa has."

"Yes, but that was a different age. Times have changed. Sooner or later, you'll have to leave."

I looked down. I could argue that lots of people — good people like Stan Olson and Willie Parker — never left, never wanted to leave. But I knew what she meant. "I know," I said.

"Neil, I'm just trying to help you get ready for that time. I wasn't sure about keeping you here for school in the fall; I hadn't made that decision yet. But I wanted you to take the first step out of Shipley this summer. My mom and dad just didn't know enough about the world to give me that help when I was your age."

"You've done okay."

"Yes, I have. But I made a lot of mistakes along the way."

"Including one particularly big one."

She smiled. "Well, I wouldn't take that one back. Not when a certain boy with a ridiculous nickname has given me so much to brag about."

"Like what?"

145

She shrugged. "A three twenty-six batting average, seven home runs, and twenty-three runs batted in."

"Twenty-two. You really pay attention to that stuff?"

"Of course. I don't tell people you're going to be the next star catcher for the Dodgers, but I do my share of proud-mama bragging."

I looked down, feeling embarrassed, pleased, and stupid. "I had no idea. . . . So what do we do now?"

"Well, I guess you could brush your teeth while I get a couple of fans going. Then we could go out for some ice cream while the place airs out."

"I'm sorry about that, Mom. That was really dumb."

"It had a certain flair. I'm going to remember it for the next time we need to get the attention of a stubborn client."

"Mom, I've got to find my own way out of Shipley. And in my own time."

She hesitated. "I know."

I wish I could say we didn't fight anymore after that evening. But we did. We argued about the job, and she even tried to get me to visit a couple of the private schools she'd investigated. Still, her heart wasn't really in it, and we reached a compromise: I'd stay another month at the job if she gave up on the school idea for that year, anyway.

I got back to Wisconsin feeling logy and out of shape after the weeks of breathing polluted air and doing nothing more physical than pushing the mail cart up and down the corridors. Never again. I might not spend my life in Shipley, but I'd be damned if I'd spend it rotting in an office building somewhere. I was going to play some ball. Starting right now.

Jeff shuffled awkwardly. "Bull, it's not like you won't get to play. But Greg's doing a helluva job for us. I can't just tell him that now you're back he's going to sit the bench for the last three weeks of the season. Besides, this isn't the old team anymore. There are a lot of new guys. They wouldn't understand."

"Well, what do you suggest, then?" I snapped.

"We'll divide things up. You, Greg, and Dave can do some switching around between first base and catcher. Everybody'll get a chance to play."

"How about you? You giving anything up?"

He shrugged. "One of you guys wants to come out and play a little short, it's okay by me."

Yeah, fat chance of that: *The Three Stooges Play Shortstop*. For a moment, I almost told him to go screw himself. I'd find another team or say to hell with baseball for the summer. But I needed to get a bat in my hands. Needed it more than I could ever remember. I watched the team going through warm-ups. "Okay," I said. "I've been in the bull pen before. Just get me one at bat today."

"Good man," he said, and jogged off to tell Keneally that everything was cool.

I'll have to hand it to Greg Fowler for half a dozen

things. He did all the things catchers are supposed to do and did them pretty well for a guy with almost no experience. And, he came to talk to me. He even offered to sit the bench, but I told him that I was willing to split things up. Before long, I was teaching him the finer points of catching. He was going to be okay, maybe even good enough to compete for backup catcher next year.

Back at the beginning of this bitch session, I said that Grandpa took no notice of me. It wasn't exactly that. He was glad to see me home, but I could tell that things had changed. He'd always given me a lot of freedom, but now that I was going to be a junior and had a driver's license, he was giving me no direction at all. Not that I needed any. It was just . . . well, a change.

A lot of the change probably had to do with Ellen Barrens, who had run the bakery downtown with her husband until he died and she'd sold it to a nephew. She was a nice lady, whom I always pictured dressed in crisp white behind the pastry counter. So it was a shock to see her gussied up and holding on to Grandpa's arm as they went off to dance at the Eagle's Club. For a lot of reasons, they seemed a perfect fit. I could see it, and I think he could, too. What that would mean in time . . . Well, I'm not sure anyone knew.

I also said that Sandi completely ignored me. Well, not quite completely. She wasn't mad at me or anything. I just wasn't on her planet very often — and Billy was all the time.

Then there were my fink neighbors. I'd been cutting lawns for a lot of them since fifth grade, so I figured they owed me some loyalty. Wrong again. Three little twerps had divided up my business in my absence. I thought briefly of doing a little strong-arm on them for part of the action. (Hey, I had the size and the nickname of a good Mafiosi.) But instead, I just left notes on the doors of all my former clients, letting them know I was back and available if they needed me. I got a few calls, but my summer income was definitely on the slide.

Coach Borsheim tipped me about the job with Parks and Rec. "Are we talking real little kids, Coach?"

"Pretty little. Six to eight."

"To me that's real, real little. What am I supposed to do with them?"

"Teach them to play catch, hit the ball a little, run the bases. No keeping score. Everybody just having a good time."

"Uh, I really don't have any experience with kids that age."

"Go ahead and try it. You'll probably enjoy it."

And I did, which in itself was pretty weird. The kids were all full of enthusiasm, never worrying if they missed a ball or a tag or a base. I enjoyed baseball, but had I ever had this much fun at it?

Jeff came by to pick me up at the end of one session. I had a kid on my shoulder, another stuck to my leg like a leech, and two or three more pulling at me as I tried to get everybody to put away bats and helmets. Jeff, who's had the twins to train him, helped get things cleaned up. When the last of the kids left with parents, he shook his head. "Bull, you never cease to amaze me. I can see you twenty years from now, fifty pounds overweight and everybody's favorite playground director."

"Hey, screw you, pal. Twenty years from now, I'm going to be hitting homer about number six hundred for the world champions."

"Then you'd better get some practice in. Speedwise especially. Ready to play some ball?"

"Always am."

I had a good fall semester. School has always come pretty easy for me, and I didn't have any problem making the honor roll. I liked my teachers, liked my classes, and generally had a pretty good time.

Like the year before, I played trombone in the marching band during football season. At our game against McArthur, we did a dueling-bands number with their band, our rows and theirs combing through each other. "Hey, Bull," somebody whispered loudly, and I had a quick sight of Bev as she swung a bass trumpet to her lips and the bands rolled into "On Wisconsin."

We caught up with each other after the game. She gave me a hug. "Gosh, you look good," she said. "You never told me you were musical. I figured you for the football-player type."

"Too much brute force. You know me, I'm the finesse type."

"Oh, yeah. I'd kind of forgotten that. Nose jobs a specialty."

"Speaking of which, how's Andy?"

"Oh, fine. Living with his girlfriend, working for my dad in the plumbing biz, playing some softball."

"And how about you?"

"Lonely, bored, could use a visit from an out-of-towner one of these days. Otherwise, I'm doing great."

Somebody in a McArthur band uniform yelled, "Hey, Bev. Come on before you miss the bus."

"Gotta scoot. Remember me, huh?"

"Sure thing." I waved as she ran for the bus. Good people, Bev.

"Who's the beefy babe?" Jeff was at my elbow, wolfing the last of a box of popcorn.

"Andy Herkert's sister. And she's not beefy, just normal sized like me. As opposed to small. Like you, for instance."

"Whatever you say. Let's go get a pizza. I'm hungry."

I got a card from Bev at Halloween — a big black cat humped up and hissing. She'd drawn a balloon from the cat's mouth and written: "Come see me or else!" But I never took it as more than teasing and didn't. At Christmas, there was a card from all the Herkerts, and Grandpa and I sent one their way. I thought I might see her when McArthur came to Shipley for a Saturday basketball game, but that was the weekend I had the flu and didn't make it any farther from my bed than the john.

Jeff and I played intramural basketball and followed our usual regimen of training for baseball. But by late February, even I started getting sick of it. "Come on, Jeff. We did weights yesterday. Why do we have to do them again today?"

He finished a curl and paused, breathing hard. "College scouts, that's why. This is the year they're going to hear about me. And I don't mean the scouts from the little schools. I want the scouts from New Mexico, Arizona, and USC. And I've got to be stronger, faster, and better for those types to pay attention to me."

I bit my lip. Yeah, that's what I wanted, too. I sat down on the weight bench and started adjusting the bench-press bar. "They'll hear about you," I said.

"Oh, yeah? Why? I hardly played last year. I'm not a pitcher, and you and I both know they're the big prize for these guys. That's why Rob McHugh got a full boat to go to USC. And that's why Phuong will get one too, if he keeps getting better. But I'm just a shortstop. And, as you like to point out, I'm not exactly a Cal Ripken-sized one, either. So I'm going to have to make up for it in some other ways." He shifted the weight to the other arm and started doing curls again. "And, by the way," he said, "if you're going to get them to pay attention to you, you're going to have to figure out how to pick up some speed."

I grunted under the weight of my third rep. "And how am I supposed to do that?"

"I don't know, but you'd better work at it."

He was right, and I did. Night after night, I ran sprints in the gym. Everyone, the basketball players in particular, made cracks about slow-motion and stop-frame action. I kept at it, always hoping for a break-through. But my time over ninety feet improved only a tenth of a second. "It's something," Jeff said, but his tone wasn't encouraging.

Sandi came down the hall with a bundle of roses over-flowing her arms. "Hi, Bull." She grinned.

"Hi, Sandi. Nice flowers."

"It's our anniversary. Eleven months. Can you believe it? It seems like just yesterday. Anyway, Billy said he just couldn't wait another month to send me flowers."

"So he sent you eleven roses instead of a dozen?"

She counted. "Oh, yeah. I hadn't noticed that. Isn't that cute?"

"Adorable," I said.

"Hey, are you still mad at us?"

"Nah, that wouldn't be the word."

"Good, because I think everybody should try to get along with everybody else. That's what I try to do."

Which, of course, made it the only way things should be. "So," I said, "do you want to go out Friday night? I think we could get along."

She stared at me. "Bull, you know I'll be going out with Billy. What makes you even ask?"

153

I held a hand to my chest. "It's just the rejection, Sandi. I'm so addicted that I can't do without it."

She laughed. "Oh, Bull. We were never right for each other. You know that."

Just how many clichés could she throw out in a minute? "Yeah, sure," I said. "You guys have a good time." I headed for the gym to see if Borsheim had posted the sign-up sheet for baseball.

He had, and I wrote my name at the top, wrote it large because this year, slow or not, I was going to make people notice me: big-college scouts, weak-kneed pitchers from places like Caledonia, and one stuck-up girl. Her, for damned sure.

SPRING — JUNIOR YEAR

FOR THE FIRST TIME IN MY LIFE, I felt like I was playing on a real championship team. We had defense, hitting, speed (with one or two exceptions), pitching, and belief. Last year, the guys from Caledonia had seemed unbeatable, but this year we knew we could take them. Not easily, but we could do it.

Jeff had a lot to do with the belief part of it. Borsheim had announced on the first day of practice that Jeff would be captain. That surprised some people because the honor had always gone to a senior before. Still, anybody who'd ever played summer league knew Jeff's rep. Only Frank Multerer tried to undercut him, calling him a hot dog and bad-mouthing him to the other seniors.

He tried it in the locker room one afternoon on big Mike Shields, our first baseman, and Charlie Worth, who'd probably get the job at second. I was changing in the next row over, and Frank didn't guess or didn't care if I overheard. "Where's Borsheim get off naming a junior. And one who didn't even start last year. We ought to get together a petition or something."

Mike slapped him down. "Look, Mule. I ain't real happy that Coach passed over some other guys. Me included. But he did and I can see why, because if everybody got off their butts and played like Hanson we might just have a shot at the championship. And I don't know about you, but I'm just a little damned sick of third and fourth place."

"Quit dreaming," Frank snapped. "Hanson's a fake. That team he's had in summer league never went anywhere. And so what if he's got a good glove? He's not going to hit for shit once the pitchers get onto him. Hell, all those hits in practice are just because his buddies are doing the pitching. Especially that little bull pen faggot, Jim what's-his-name."

My vision went red, and I stepped around the row of lockers, my right hand already reaching for the back of Frank's skinny neck. He spun, the color going from his face. He tried to sneer, but it didn't work. Mike stepped between us. "Just hold it right there, Bull," he growled. "This is a senior problem, and we'll work it out."

I hesitated and then lowered my hand. "Okay, Mike. But if he ever calls Jim a faggot again, I'm going to rip his head off and use his spine for a pencil."

"Yeah? Well, just back off for now. We all know the Mule's got a mouth on him. Let us handle this."

I gave Frank a dead-eyed stare. "Okay, but just this time."

With Jeff running things on the field, Borsheim had become almost relaxed. Most days, he left the defense to Jeff and the pitchers to me, so he could concentrate on hitting. And he was a good batting coach, although I got a little sick of him yelling, "Contact, contact, contact."

Three days before our first game, he called Jeff and me into his office to show us the lineup. He'd let the scrimmage roster settle down in the past few days, and there weren't any surprises. "So," Borsheim said, "who gets the start, Bull?"

I took a breath. "That depends if you want to go with seniority or the best pitcher, Coach."

"What'd be your choice?"

On the spot again. Damn, I hated it when he did that. "I've always preferred winning games to worrying about egos. So, I'd start the year with Phuong and let him pitch as many games as he can. Frank's a good pitcher and he'll get his share of wins, but he ain't Phuong."

"Okay. You've got your one-two. We'll need a third starter a few times, especially if the schedule gets screwed up with rain days. Who's it going to be? Stroetz?"

157

"I'd rather just use him in relief, Coach. I think we should go with Ed Parkenham."

He raised his eyebrows. "My lord Parkenham?"

I smiled. Edward Albert Parkenham III, sophomore pitcher and twenty-third in line (so he said) to inherit the Earldom of Parkenham somewhere in England, was a few flakes short of shovelful. "Yes, sir. He's got all the equipment. He just needs a lot of practice."

"Okay, you're the expert. So, how's our friend the Mule going to take being number two?"

"Not well. As a matter of fact, he is going to be royally pissed."

He nodded. "Well, I'll talk to him. Okay, here's one small surprise: I'm not putting another catcher on the varsity. Keneally can handle the bull pen, and Fowler and Kaiser are better off splitting up time on the jayvees. So if you get hurt in a game, there's a certain shortstop who's going to make a rapid transformation."

"Lord, I'd better stay healthy," I said.

"Coach, I'm no damned good at that stuff —" Jeff blurted.

Borsheim held up a hand. "As a matter of fact, you are. You're not Halloway and you're not the Bull, but you'll do." He glanced at his watch. "My wife's complaining about me getting home late every night, and I've still got to talk to our problem child. We'll see you tomorrow."

Leaving the locker room twenty minutes later, we heard shouting in Borsheim's office. The next morning, word was that Frank had quit the team. But he went crawling back to Borsheim that afternoon.

We opened against Lein's Forks, the team that had beaten us out for second. Our offense knocked their starter out in the first inning with five runs, and we went on from there to win, 10–2. Phuong was terrific for five innings, which was enough for a first game, and Borsheim put in Phil Stroetz to finish up.

We beat Mosinee in our second game. Jeff and I both hit homers to help Frank get his first win, 7–3. "Since when," I said to Jeff after the game, "do you do that shit?"

"Since this year. I'm up eight pounds, and I'm going to hit a home run for every pound."

"Your mother, you are. Stick to the line drives, wimp."

He grinned. "What's the matter? You afraid of a little competition?"

"From Joe Spence, maybe. Not from you."

If I'd been paying attention to something in my life besides baseball, I might have noticed that Grandpa and Ellen Barrens were getting *real* friendly. Instead, I just walked in on that reality unawares. Or almost.

Borsheim called off practice on a Tuesday, so that he and Haight could go to Mrs. Saxon's retirement party. Usually, a few of us would have knocked a ball around on our own, but for one reason or another, everybody decided to take the afternoon off. So, I showed up at home shortly after three, something I hadn't done since long before the snow melted.

Mrs. B.'s blue Mercury was standing in the driveway, and I expected to find the two of them sitting at the kitchen table, drinking coffee and playing cribbage. But they weren't, and dumbshit me, I just followed the sound of their voices. Until, that is, I came to the closed bedroom door. Inside, Mrs. B. laughed. "Oh, I like old men. Especially ones with beards and hairy chests." I couldn't make out Grandpa's deep rumble, but he must have said something complimentary, because she laughed and said, "Oh, get on with you. Not since some things headed south."

I backed up slowly, careful not to trip over the cat. (We didn't have a cat, but you know what I mean.)

I went for a long walk and talk with myself. Because I'll admit it, I was flabbergasted. I don't know why exactly. Grandpa loved women and made no secret about it. Yet somehow, I'd never really imagined that he did more than dance and flirt with them. But here it was, the middle of the afternoon, and Grandpa and Mrs. B. were in the sack together! Oh, Lord, the world was a hell of a lot more complicated than it used to be.

Billy was in a howling fury. "Goddamn it, Bull! Is she there?"

"Who?" I said, knowing full well who.

"Sandi, damn it. Where is she?"

I leaned back in Grandpa's recliner. "I don't keep track of her, Billy."

"Bull, so help me. If she's over there and you lay a hand —"

"Billy, don't do that. Don't make threats you damn well know you can't back up."

"Look, you big —"

"Billy, *don't*."

He paused, fuming. Finally, he managed to level his voice. "She's not there, huh?"

"I told you that."

"And she wasn't there this afternoon?"

"You didn't ask that, but she wasn't."

"And you haven't heard from her?"

"Nope."

Suddenly, he was on the edge of tears. "Bull, she told me that I don't love her enough and that she was going to go see somebody who did. And when I tried —"

I sighed. "Just hold it, Billy. I don't care. I am not involved."

He paused, sniffling. "Bull, if you see her, would you tell her —"

"No, Billy, I won't tell her anything. Because I don't give a rat's ass what happens to either of you." I hung up, leaned back, and stared at Sandi. "And you," I said, "can leave."

She didn't move from the corner of the couch. "Why?

161

Isn't this what you've always wanted? Aren't you the guy who called me up every week for about six years?"

"With some exaggeration on the length of my insanity, yes. But I didn't call you this time."

She watched me, her eyes cool. "But I'm here. Are you going to take a chance or not?"

And goddamn it, I was tempted. Tempted, because I'd always figured if I could just get my arms around her for ten minutes, I could wake her up to what we could be together. "No," I said. "Because this isn't about you and me. This is about you and Billy."

"Bull," she said, her voice shifting to that little-girl whine, "I really want to be with you."

"Oh, horseshit, Sandi. You're going to use me to tie that poor SOB in knots and then you're either going to take him back or tell both of us to kiss your ass. And I'm not going to do it. Not now, not then. Now get the hell out of here."

For another long moment, she didn't move. Then she gave me her brightest smile. "Well, you can't say that I never gave you the chance. 'Night, now."

I closed the door behind her and watched through the window as she sashayed down the walk, giving me a lot of hip to watch. And I wanted to hit things, break things, tear doors off their hinges. But instead, I let two tears, my first since Grandma's death, well up in my eyes. Damn it, if she could just feel a hundredth part of what I felt . . .

* * *

They had long memories in McArthur. They booed my name when the lineups were announced and booed me in person when I led off the top of the second.

"Better not dig in, jerk," Pat Wilson, their catcher, muttered.

I didn't say anything, just kept my eye on the pitcher, a red-headed senior I'd never seen before. He leaned in for the sign, nodded, and looped a curve low and away for a ball. He threw another curve, this one nicking the outside corner for a strike. Shit, I could have handled that one. I stepped out, got my concentration again, and stood back in. And after throwing two outside, he went for my head. I felt the wind against my face as I bailed out.

I got up, dusted off, and stepped back in without a word. In a way, I had this coming, and I'd be damned if they'd hear me whine. I slapped an outside pitch foul down the first baseline. 2–2. If he was going to do it again, he'd do it now. He did, aiming thigh-high this time. I let it hit me.

He had some good heat, and it stung like hell, but I didn't let that show as I jogged down to first where Phuong was coaching. "You okay, Bull?"

"Yep. Might have to steal a base to get back at Big Red out there."

"God, don't try that. Borsheim'd blame me."

I took my standard two-step lead as Mike Shields stood in. He slapped the second pitch to short, and I was pounding toward second. The shortstop tagged the bag

163

himself, paused a heartbeat to gauge the trajectory, then fired the throw to first at my head. I slid below it, hopped up, and jogged toward our bench along the third baseline. Borsheim was on his feet. "If they pull one more stunt like that, I'm going to lodge a protest."

"Forget it, Coach," I said. "They're just making a point."

Con Richards fouled off a half dozen pitches before working Red for a walk, which gave me time to study the faces in the stands. No Bev, just a lot of hostility.

Tom Rice bounced to first for the third out, and we went on defense. I warmed up Frank, who was in a better mood than usual, probably figuring I'd get hit two or three times before the end of the game. Their first batter was a lefty, which meant he had to face Frank's snake-mean slider breaking in on him. We got two quick strikes with sliders, and I called a fastball on the outside half to finish him off. Instead, Frank threw one at the kid's ankles, forcing him to dance out of the way. I looked at Frank hard. He shrugged. I called the outside fastball again, and again he threw at the kid's ankles, causing more fancy footwork and bringing a chorus of boos from the McArthur fans.

Before the ump could say anything, I jogged out to the mound. "What the hell are you doing, Frank?"

"Trying to get a strike. I just missed with a couple."

"Horseshit. You never miss with that pitch."

"Well, hell, Bull. That red-headed kid's been throwing at you. I'm just getting a little payback."

164

"When it's time for payback, I'll tell you. Right now, we're just trying to win a ball game."

He shrugged. "You're the boss."

"Damned right I am. Fastball, outside half, at the belt. Got it?"

"Hey, I got it."

I jogged back to the plate and crouched. And the SOB tried to kneecap the kid.

"That's it!" the umpire snapped. "One more and —"

"There aren't going to be any more," I said. I stood, took a couple of steps to my left, and held out my mitt for an intentional ball. Frank stared at me. I shook the mitt, and reluctantly he lobbed one in. The batter jogged down to first, and their right-handed shortstop stepped in. I didn't even look at our bench and Borsheim. Instead, I stepped out to the right and called for another intentional ball. Frank looked helplessly at our bench and then threw it.

Borsheim was off the bench and striding to the mound. He gestured to me, and I jogged out. "Okay," he said, "what's going on?"

"Frank can't seem to read my signs, so I'm calling the only pitch I know he can throw where I want him to."

Borsheim glared at Frank. "That true?"

"Coach, they've been throwing at Bull —"

"Did I tell you to retaliate?"

"Well, no —"

"Did he?"

"No."

"Then don't. Now go to work or I'll sit you down. And not just for this game."

Frank behaved himself after that, and slowly the buzz from the stands settled. We got out of the inning with a strikeout and a double-play ground ball.

I came to bat again in the top of the fourth with us leading three–zip. I glanced at Wilson when he got down in his catcher's crouch. He shrugged his shoulders. "That was a class act a couple of innings ago. We're satisfied if you are."

"I'm just here to play ball. I never wanted to fight."

"Okay. Let's see if you can hit some of Red's smoke."

Curve, I thought, and did the smoking myself, lashing it into the right-field corner for a double that Jeff would, of course, tell me should have been a triple.

We won 5–2, making our record 6–0 for the season. After the game, I looked again for Bev. No luck. I ought to write her sometime. Just for fun.

Halfway through an almost perfect spring, we were an almost perfect nine and one. Stockfarm had gotten lucky and beaten us 3–1 with some fantastic pitching from Jim Graveen, a nobody senior reliever making his first varsity start. Too bad he hadn't had his one great game against the guys from Caledonia, who'd casually rung up a 10–0 start. They'd be coming down in two more games. Then we'd see who the big dogs really were.

Grandpa's attendance had been spotty, so I wasn't

surprised when he didn't come to see us rack up win number ten that Saturday with a 9–2 thumping of Walthrop. I was still pumped up when I got home, anxious to tell him how I'd coaxed Ed Parkenham through five innings for his first win, how Jeff had made the greatest over-the-shoulder catch I'd ever seen by a shortstop, and how I'd blasted my eighth homer over the scoreboard in dead center field. (Ever modest, I would, of course, wait until he asked before describing that spectacular feat.)

But I forgot all those things when I saw him hunched over the kitchen table, his face sweaty and gray. "Grandpa, are you okay?"

He tried to smile. "Oh, probably. But maybe you'd better take me over to the clinic. Just to be sure."

"What is it? Your heart?"

"Just indigestion, I think."

"Maybe I ought to call an ambulance."

"No, that'll just rile up the neighbors. Before you know it, they'll start bringing us cakes and stews and what all else. Hell, we had enough to feed an army when your grandma died." He started getting up, holding his left arm tight against his chest.

"Grandpa —"

"Neil, let's just go."

I fussed around him as he climbed into the car. I backed out fast, and he said, "Whoa, boy. Nice and easy. Nothing's going to happen between here and there, except maybe you getting us killed."

The receptionist spoke into a telephone, and a minute later, a nurse and an attendant with a wheelchair came hurrying down the hall. "Which one of you is having the chest pains?" the nurse snapped. I pointed to Grandpa, and the attendant spun the chair around, plopped him into it, and they were off, the nurse already asking him stern questions.

I answered what questions I could for the receptionist, and then sat in the far corner of the lobby, staring through the windows at the sunny afternoon. Green grass and blue sky had never looked so good, and I'd never been so scared.

Forty-five minutes later, the doctor called me into his office. "Your grandfather's resting comfortably. He suffered a myocardial infarction, what is generally called a heart attack. We gave him some medication to steady his heart rhythm and to ease the pain."

"Is he going to be okay?"

"Oh, I think so, but we'll keep him in intensive care for a couple of days. By then, we'll know how best to get him on his feet again. You can go in and see him now."

Grandpa was lying on his back, his eyes closed and his face ashen. An IV tube ran from a plastic bag to his wrist, and a humming machine stood by his bed, its sensors pasted on his chest. He opened his eyes and smiled wanly at me. "Well, did I scare the hell out of you, Grandson? Sure scared the hell out of myself."

I sat down, awkwardly putting a hand on his. "Yeah, it was scary, but the doctor says you're going to be okay."

"Sure," he said. "Gonna have to avoid all excitement, that's all. No late nights, no dancing, no chasing after wild women."

"Nah, he didn't really say that."

He smiled faintly. "No, not yet . . . So, did you win?"

For a second, I couldn't think what he was talking about. "Oh. Yeah, we did. Ed Parkenham got his first win, I hit a home run, and Jeff made a couple of nice plays."

He closed his eyes. "That's great . . . Did you call your mother yet?"

"Not yet. I didn't want to scare her until I knew what was going on."

"Well, call her when you get home. Then have a good supper and get to bed in decent season. No sense in missing any school over this."

"Grandpa, it's Saturday. Besides, you don't have to worry about me."

"No, of course I don't. It's just easier than worrying about myself." He swallowed hard, a trickle of moisture leaking from the corners of his eyes.

"It's going to be okay, Grandpa. Really."

He gave my hand a squeeze. "Sure. Get on your way, now."

* * *

Mom moves fast in a crisis. She caught a red-eye from LA to Minneapolis, the first morning flight into Mosinee, and swung her rent-a-car into our driveway while the church bells were ringing on Sunday morning.

When we got to the hospital, Grandpa was sitting up, but his skin was pale and the gray stubble on his cheeks made him look a hundred years old. He smiled, reaching out a hand for Mom. "There's my honey."

She took his hand and leaned over to kiss him on the cheek. "Hello, Dad. How are you feeling?"

"All right. My butt's sore, but they tell me I've got to stay in bed."

"Well, you cooperate. I feel sorry for these nurses already."

"Oh, I'm no trouble. Hell, I sleep most of the time."

They went on talking. I excused myself after a while, got a can of pop from the machine in the lobby, and went for a walk around half a dozen blocks. She was waiting in the lobby when I got back. "He's going to take a nap, have lunch, and then watch a ball game. I told him we'd come back to see him before supper."

"How do you think he is?"

"I think he's doing fine, considering. Just like you are and I am."

By that afternoon, Mom had taken over our living room and was consulting files from her briefcase, tapping away at her laptop, and waiting for her skypager to beep, Sunday afternoon or not.

Phuong, Jeff, and Jim came over, and we threw a ball around in the backyard. After asking how Grandpa was doing, they seemed to want to talk about something else. "Billy and Sandi are back together," Jeff said, giving me a sidelong look to gauge my reaction.

"Didn't notice they were apart," I said.

"Uh-huh," he said.

"Maybe we ought to get a bat and go down to the park," Jim said. "We could play some five hundred."

"Yeah," Phuong said. "Come on."

I hesitated. "I've got to ask my mom."

Jeff grinned. "Tell her she can play, too. I still remember when she used to."

"You've got a hell of a memory. I'll see you down there in a few minutes."

She let me go on the promise that I'd be back in an hour so we could go to the hospital. On impulse, I asked her if she actually would like to play some ball. She looked up from the screen of her laptop, a quizzical smile on her face. "No, thanks. But if you've got a game this week, I'll come and embarrass you with my proud-mama act."

On Tuesday, while the guys were clubbing Walthrop around 10–4 in the return game, the doctors ran a tube into Grandpa's heart to ream out two blocked arteries. Angioplasty, they called it, but fancy name or not, the whole idea gave me the creeps.

Mom and I sat in the sunny waiting room. She had

171

her laptop, but it lay unopened beside her. "It's okay if you work, Mom," I said. "I've got something to read."

She waved a hand. "Work doesn't seem very interesting right now."

"Somebody's got to pay the doctor's bills."

"That's all taken care of. Your grandfather has first-rate health insurance. And so do you. I saw to that a long time ago." She spent a long minute staring at the floor, lips pursed. "Neil, what happens if he dies?"

"But, Mom, the doctor said —"

"I don't mean today. He'll come through this just fine. But sometime in the next year or two. Before you're of age and can decide how to make your own way."

I hesitated. "Are we going to start talking about LA again?"

"Don't you think we ought to?"

"We went through all that last summer. I don't want to live in LA."

"Why not, Neil? LA isn't so bad. I know you were bored last summer. But I was going through a very busy period. Now we're bringing in another associate, and I'd have more time for you."

It occurred to me that this conversation was going in a very strange direction, considering that Grandpa was, so far, very much alive. "Mom, I love you, but I just couldn't do it. Not even if Grandpa died, and I couldn't stay in the house anymore. I know Jeff's folks would let me stay with them."

"Do you think that would be fair to them? They've

got Jeff and the two little ones. They've got lots to worry about already."

"I know, but I'm real good with the kids."

"Still . . ." She let it trail off.

For a long couple of minutes, we sat in silence, caught — as always — at odds. "I'm sorry, Mom," I said.

She nodded and looked away, the afternoon sunlight catching the gray streaks in her hair.

We could tie Caledonia for the league lead with a win, and for the first time in memory, the stands in Shipley were filled for a game. Even the guys from Caledonia, where they filled the stands every game, looked impressed. Sandi had gotten the junior cheerleaders together, and they were doing their best to grab some of the attention. (Unkind of me? Well, what can I say?)

Caledonia must have had the pitching machine set to slider all week in practice, because they absolutely killed Frank's. He was gone in three, and they pounded on Stroetz for three innings, building a 6–1 lead. It could just as easily have been 10–1, if Billy hadn't climbed the fence to rob Joe Spence of a grand slam for the third out in the top of the sixth.

Jeff caught up with me as I trudged toward the bench. "How about bringing in Phuong next inning?"

"We're five down with an inning and a half to go, and we've got McArthur coming in on Monday."

"To hell with them. We can catch these guys."

"You think so, huh?"

"Damn right I think so."

I gazed into his fierce blue eyes. "Okay, let's ask Borsheim."

Borsheim stared at us. "Not good management," he said. "Just warming up a starter takes two or three innings out of his arm. Which means I'll have two tired starters and my best reliever beat up on Monday. Then who am I going to pitch against McArthur?"

"Coach, give us a chance," Jeff pleaded. "I know we can do it."

Borsheim hesitated, and then looked at me. "Can you win with Parkenham on Monday?"

"Yeah, I can win with him, Coach. We might have to go to the bull pen early, but we'll get it done."

"Okay," he said. "Get three runs back this inning, and I'll bring in the Tiger."

We spread the word, and then went out to get the three runs. It was tough, but we managed with a mix of singles, stolen bases, sacrifices, and a big double by Jeff.

Borsheim kept his promise. In the top of the seventh, Phuong was perfect, his fastball breaking five inches to hit the center of my mitt every time. Three up, three down, three K's. We were still down two runs, and Caledonia brought in a new pitcher to get the last three outs. He was a little fart who didn't look old enough to be in high school. But, Lord, did he have stuff. He blew Billy away on three straight fastballs, then paralyzed Carl with curves for a second strikeout.

Jeff knocked the weighted doughnut off his bat as I came to the on-deck circle. "Who the hell is that kid?" he growled.

"We just figured it out. He's Rob McHugh's little brother, Jamie. He's a ninth-grader, for God's sake."

"Oh, shit. If Rob taught him half his pitches, I'll never hit him cold."

"Let's play some ball, boys," the umpire called.

"I'm going to see if he can field," Jeff said.

Jeff took a stinging fastball for a strike and then squared as the kid came in with another. Jeff killed it, dragging it down the third baseline. The McHugh kid could field, but not as well as Jeff could run, and his throw was late by a step and a half.

Gary Melcher called time and jogged in from second to remind McHugh who'd be covering the bag if Jeff tried to steal.

I swung the weighted bat over my head a final time as Mike came to the on-deck circle. "Get the word to Jeff to give me two pitches," I said. "Then he can run."

"Gotcha," Mike said.

I stepped into the batter's box. I grinned at their catcher, Jake Polster. "How you doing, Jake?"

"Feels good to win. How you doin'?"

"Never better." I looked out at the kid. "Hey, McHugh, how's the big brother?" I called.

The kid looked surprised. "Uh, fine. Real good."

I dug a little hole for my back foot. "He enjoying college?"

"Yeah, I think so."

"Glad to hear it. Jeez, I guess that must have been just a rumor that he got suspended for doing something over in the primate lab with . . ." I looked at Polster. "Do you remember what it was, Jake? Some kind of baboon, wasn't it?"

"Shut the hell up and play ball," Polster said.

"Come on, Jake. Just because you and the baboon were related —"

"Ump, we gotta listen to this?"

"Come on, play ball," the umpire said.

"Okay, okay," I said. I grinned at the kid again. "I hit one out off your brother last year. Did you see that one? Went out left center on the climb."

The kid ignored me, read Polster's sign, and came to the stretch. And I knew exactly where the fastball was going to be and it was and I hit it. Hit it so damned hard, I could feel every bone in my body vibrate. But I didn't get any loft on it at all. Out in left, Joe Spence cruised back, timed his leap, and got it a foot above the fence.

Final score: 6–4. And it wasn't really that close.

Everybody was quiet in the locker room. We'd seen a real championship team, and we still didn't measure up. When I could finally manage it, I said to Jeff, "I'm sorry. I —"

"Sorry for what? Hell, you hit it right on the screws."

"But I didn't get any height on it."

"And a lot of the other guys didn't hit the ball at all.

That McHugh kid's good, but he's going to have night-mares about you and me."

Borsheim came out of his office and called for quiet. "Well, we almost did it. We scrapped like hell and just fell a little short. Now our job is to stay as close to them as we can, so when we go over there at the end of the season, we'll be playing for more than just pride. Because we're gonna take 'em next time. Right?"

We tried to cheer that, but it came out faint. Borsheim compressed his lips. "Okay," he said, "McArthur's in on Monday. They're tough, so let's be ready to play."

"Always," Jeff said beside me, but even his brag didn't have its usual edge.

When Jeff let me off at home, I paused for a minute on the sidewalk before going in. Grandpa had been home from the hospital for a couple of days, and Mom was keeping up a determinedly cheerful atmosphere. If I went in with a long face now, she'd land all over me with a lecture on "priorities." So, I braced up and went in smiling. Grandpa was sitting at the kitchen table, looking almost his old self. He smiled. Mom turned from getting a dish from the microwave, and she smiled. And since I was already smiling, we were all smiling. Well, happy, happy, joy, joy.

Actually, I think Grandpa's smile was genuine — relief for getting home, relief for being alive. He was the one who got us relaxed and actually cheered up that night. And watching him joking and laughing only a week after having a heart attack made me wonder again just how we'd ever get along without him.

Mom delayed her escape from Shipley long enough to come to the game against McArthur. She came to root, too, wearing one of my baseball caps and a "Go Hornets" T-shirt. When I came out to warm up Ed Parkenham, she nudged the woman next to her and shrilled, "That's my baby." I cringed and she waved.

The rest of the team might have been down after the loss to Caledonia, but Edward Albert Parkenham III was sky high. "Calm down, Ed," I told him. "You're gonna float right off this damned mound."

He bobbed his head and grinned his goofy grin. "My arm's on fire, man, and I've got some serious smoke for these dudes. Watch out, I might just pitch a no-hitter."

"Don't ever say that! It is very bad luck. Now, listen . . ." I managed to keep him focused enough to go over the signs.

Ed doesn't have a great fastball like Phuong or a mean slider to go with a mean personality like Frank. But he does one thing very well: he keeps the ball down. Carl, Jeff, Charlie, and Mike were very busy as one McArthur batter after another beat it into the ground.

I half expected Mom to produce pom-poms from her handbag the first time I came to bat, but she confined herself to whoops and shouts of "Come on, Neil!"

Wilson, the McArthur catcher, looked at me. "Neil? Is that your real name?"

"That's it."

"Huh. I didn't expect anything so wimpy. I had you figured for a Thor or a Rocky or at least a Burt. So, who's the babe, anyway? Kind of old for you, ain't she?"

"That's my mother, stupid."

"Huh. Foxy mama. Want heat or a deuce?"

"Deuce, belt high, dead center."

He gave me a fastball out and away, but I got enough of it to drop a looping single inside the right-field foul line to score Billy from third.

Enough of McArthur's ground balls got through the infield to get them a run in the second and a run again in the fourth. But by then, we'd rung up six, and Borsheim put the Mule in to finish up.

Just before I went in to catch the top of the sixth, Mom came to the fence behind our bench. "Gotta go, dear, or I'll miss my plane. Give me a kiss." Obediently, I gave her cheek a peck through the chain link. She smiled at me radiantly. "I left some spending money on your bed. You be a good boy."

"Sure, Mom. Uh, I've gotta go play ball now."

"Make your mama proud. Remember, I was a Shipley Hornet once, too."

"Once a Hornet, always a Hornet."

"You bet," she said, waved, and hurried for her rented car.

Wilson stepped into the batter's box. "You sure that was really your mama?"

"Come on, Patsy," I said. "Let's play some ball. And I

179

wouldn't dig in, if I were you. The Mule ain't real happy about coming out of the pen to finish up. Beneath his dignity."

"Oh, I know the Mule. And a mean SOB he is. I wouldn't think of digging in."

Pat popped up as the Mule recorded the first of a half dozen easy outs. Final score: 7–2, to make us eleven and two on the year.

Caledonia lost to Lein's Forks by a run and, two games later, to our buddies from McArthur by two. (God, I loved those guys.) So, with three games and a week to go in the season, we were an identical 15–2. Borsheim reminded us again and again that we had to beat Sullivan Mills first, or the big game against Caledonia wouldn't mean crap. Still, it was hard not to look ahead.

Greg Fowler was now my regular backup, and I let him handle infield practice the day before the game against the Mills, while I worked in the pen with Ed Parkenham, who was scheduled to make his second start. The Mule was hanging around, in an even fouler mood than usual because Borsheim had taken the start away from him so his arm would be fresh for relief work in the Caledonia game.

I had my back turned, and missed seeing Billy and Greg get tangled up in a play at the plate. Billy came up holding his right arm. "Oooh, little Billy's got an owie," Frank said to no one in particular.

"How you doing, Collins?" Borsheim called from the bench.

"Okay, Coach. Just hit my funny bone."

"Come over here and let me look."

"No, it's okay, Coach."

"Collins! Get over here." Reluctantly, Billy went. Borsheim pushed up his sleeve. "Hey, what the blue hell is this?"

"Nothing, Coach." Billy tried to pull away.

"The hell it's nothing. Let me look."

"Oh, crap," Jim said at my side. "I thought I saw Billy skip his shower yesterday."

"Why?" the Mule asked. "That girl of his been givin' him hickeys? I hear she keeps him pretty well serviced."

I took a step and hit him, palm open, heel of the hand square on the sternum. He sat down hard. I stuck a finger in his face. "For once in your life, Mule, just shut up." Which was a little stupid to say, seeing he couldn't have talked at that moment to save his life. But his eyes were wide, and he managed a little nod.

I turned back to watch the scene. Coach Haight had taken over, while Borsheim led Billy off behind the equipment shed. He was quizzing him hard, but it didn't look like Billy was answering much. Out at short, Jeff signaled for a replacement. One of the jayvee infielders was only too happy to oblige. Grimly, Jeff set off to join Billy and Borsheim.

"Bull, maybe you —"

"No, Jim. I'm not involved anymore. You go ahead if you want to."

He gave me a wounded look and went. I turned to the Mule. "Get up, put your hands on your knees, and breathe deep. You'll feel better. Come on, Ed. Let's see some more of your stuff."

Borsheim called me into his office. "Why didn't you tell me about Collins and his old man?"

"I thought it was under control, Coach. And besides, Billy is not my problem these days."

"What affects this team is your problem and my problem. You should have told me."

I shook my head. "No, Coach. You made Jeff captain and he's got the Billy watch. I am not involved."

"So there's a problem between you and Collins? What is it?"

"It's personal."

"A girl?" I didn't answer, and he leaned back and closed his eyes. "Oh, hell," he said. "Something else we don't need."

"Is there anything more, Coach? I've got some things to do."

"No. Get out of here."

So the cops visited the Collins' home again. And again, Billy's old man denied everything, and this time Billy backed him up, because nothing that had come out of the deal with the court the last time had done any good. That's as much as I let Jeff tell me.

We beat Sullivan Mills, but had to come from behind to do it. Borsheim brought in Frank in the fifth, and even though we were three runs down, the Mule twice crossed up the signs, firing fastballs at my face. I was about to go out and break his arm when Jeff called time, jogged in, said between five and ten words to him, and jogged back to his position. Jeff and I weren't talking much because of the Billy thing, so I never learned exactly what he said, but the Mule was as cooperative as a lamb after that.

Saturday. We rode yelling, singing, and chanting through the May morning on the ride to Caledonia. Mostly it was just a lot of noise, but we needed it because we were pumped to the point of exploding. This time, we were going to take them. We got still when the bus turned off the main highway and rolled down into Caledonia. Carloads of teenagers pointed and hooted at the sight of the bus. A banner stretched over the street billowed in a stiff breeze: "GO CARDINALS. CHAMPS AGAIN IN '96."

"They sure take their baseball seriously here," Jeff said.

"Yeah," I said. "Real seriously." I reached a hand over the seat to touch Phuong's shoulder. "How you doing, Tiger?"

"Let me puke a few times, and I'll be fine."

"Hey, just don't think until you get on the mound. Come to think of it, don't even start then. I'll do the thinking for both of us."

We turned in at the high school and pulled up at the field. A crew from the TV station in Lein's Forks taped us getting off the bus. The reporter grabbed Borsheim and sized up the rest of us. Jeff said, "Mike, you do it. You've been on varsity longest."

Mike shrugged. "Sure, why not?"

I gave Jeff a dig in the ribs. "Hey, big league prospects aren't supposed to pass up interviews. You should have taken it. Or at least let me."

"I'm not worried about any interviews except with those guys." He pointed toward a corner of the stands, where a couple of guys with clipboards were shooting the breeze.

"You know 'em?" I asked.

"Arizona State and New Mexico. Good schools."

"Oh, yeah," I said. "The best." And again I felt envy twist my guts. I was hitting .338 with twelve home runs and twenty-six ribbies. How come they never wanted to talk to me? Damn it, today they were going to pay attention. I'd see to it.

Joe Spence drifted over during warm-ups. "Heard you got one against the Mills. That make twelve?"

"Yeah. Same as you, right?"

"Yep. We did this once in summer league, didn't we?"

"You won by one that time. This time it's my turn."

"Could be, but I'll try not to let it happen. Have a good game."

"You, too," I said, wishing him otherwise, of course. Joe? He probably did wish me well. When you're that good, you can afford to be charitable. Me, I hadn't proved that about myself just yet.

Phuong was ready, and I crouched to take his warm-ups. Phuong was having a hell of a year. Of our sixteen wins and two losses, he had exactly half of each. (Frank was 5–1, with the other three victories going to our pen.) Phuong's eyes were cold fire that day as his arm flashed over the top to lay the fastballs sizzling across the plate. God, I loved this, loved the minutes before the game, when I knew as sure as anything that my pitcher was ready and that I was ready. Okay, you bums, bring it on.

There's only so much you can say about a pitchers' duel. Hank Lutz matched Phuong strike for strike and out for out. Joe Spence got us for a double in the second and Hank himself got on with a single in the third, but that was all. Things were just as scanty for our side.

After striking out my first time, I came up again in the fourth. I said "hi" to Jake Polster, who still didn't seem to like me, leveled my bat, and called out to Hank: "Same sequence as last time will do fine, Hank. Think I got it figured out."

Hank grinned, knowing better than to get into a

conversation. He wound up and hissed a slider at my knees for a strike. Nice pitch. Probably felt so good he'd throw it again. He did and I went low to get it, golfing it into the right center-field gap. Normally, that would have been just a long single for me, but I put on all the speed I had and slid into second just ahead of the throw.

I called time to brush the dirt off my uniform. Gary Melcher eyed me. "You gained a step, Bull? Don't remember you getting out here that fast before."

"Actually, I've lost a couple, Gary. Have this calf muscle bothering me. Usually, I'd leg that into a triple."

"Uh-huh. And my granny runs a forty in four point two."

"Slow old bag, ain't she?" I clapped my hands. "Come on, Mike. Let's do it."

Mike came through, blasting a shot off the fence in deep left center. I made it all the way home, holding out a palm to get a five from Polster as I crossed the plate. He ignored me.

Even with Phuong pitching, a single run wasn't much. Caledonia tied the game in their half of the inning on another double by Joe Spence, a fielder's choice, and a sac fly. We were going to have to work harder.

We got another chance in the top of the sixth, when Jeff singled with one out and stole second. I came up and hit a Hank curve hard. But I knew even as I dropped the bat that I'd gotten under it just a hair too much to overcome the breeze blowing in from left. Joe Spence loped back, set himself, and caught it with his back against the fence. I could see him grinning even at that distance.

We were still tied at a run apiece going into the bottom of the seventh. And I knew exactly how the rest of the game would go just as surely as if I'd seen the videotape already. Phuong would get them this inning — maybe easy, maybe hard — but he'd get them to send the game into extra innings. I'd come up after Jeff in the top of the eighth, and this time I was going to blast one that Joe Spence couldn't catch. I could already see it going, see Joe's shoulders sag as he pulled up to watch it sail over the fence. And even if that was the only run we scored, we'd win, because they weren't going to score any more on us. Not the way Phuong was pitching.

But first we had to get them in the bottom of the seventh. Dale Warren struck out without any fuss, but we had some nasty luck against Hank, who blooped a double down the right-field line. Robbie Miller moved Hank to third with a slow roller to Charlie Worth at second. I thought they'd pinch hit for Gary Melcher, but after hesitating a moment, Caledonia's coach gestured him toward the plate. And I relaxed a bit, because as far as I was concerned, Gary was good glove, no hit, no problem.

I glanced up the line at Lutz, as Gary stepped into the box. "How you doin', Gary?"

"Fine, Bull. And please shut up."

"Sure," I said. "Just being friendly. That's how I always think of baseball. All sports, really. You know, just

187

a chance to be friendly and make friends. Don't you agree?"

"No."

I grinned and, reminding myself that Hank Lutz *was* only ninety feet from the plate, decided that I really should shut up. Phuong leaned in for the sign, and I waggled one finger — no sense messing around, bring on the heat. Phuong reared back and his arm came forward like a whip, the ball a white blur out of his hand. Gary made a small, frightened sound and missed. And so did I. That's all there really is to say, I simply missed the damned thing.

I lunged after the ball as it rolled toward the backstop. I swept it up and fired it toward the spot where I knew Phuong would be covering home. But I was too late. Hank slid in, taking Phuong's legs out from under him in the split second before the ball got there, and the ump's arms flew out in the safe sign. For a long moment, nobody seemed to move. Then Gary and the other Caledonia kids piled on Hank, finally lifting him to their shoulders. Hell, it should have been me they were carrying from the field. Very slowly, I took off my mask and let it drop at my feet.

Phuong trudged over. "Come on, Bull. It's over. No point standing around."

I looked past him to where Jeff still stood at short, hands on hips, his face expressionless as he watched the celebration. He shook himself, pulled off his glove, and examined his fingers. Then he jogged off the field, pulled his equipment bag from under the bench, and started packing up. And I just couldn't go over to him, couldn't apologize yet for losing what had meant more to him than anyone.

"Hey, Bull, come on," Phuong said.

With two victories against us, Caledonia had won the conference no matter what happened in the last game of the year. We played ours against New Oxford on the last day of school for seniors. Frank Multerer pitched his farewell game, holding them down to just one run on four hits. My two home runs were more than enough offense in a 5–1 victory. But, I swear, playing that game when everybody in the stands knew I'd lost us the championship was the hardest thing I'd ever done.

After we'd showered and changed, Jeff and I walked across the parking lot. Frank pulled out ahead of us, pausing to roll down his window. "Hey, Larsen," he yelled. "Doesn't make any difference how many homers you hit, you're still a busher and you'll always be a busher." He slammed his foot on the gas and peeled out.

"Jerk," Jeff muttered.

"Yeah," I said. But that didn't mean Frank wasn't right.

Not that it made a hell of a lot of difference to me, but Joe Spence hit two homers in Caledonia's victory over Walthrop, giving him fourteen on the year, the same as me. But his had gone toward winning a championship.

SUMMER AGAIN

THE CALEDONIA GAME PLAYED IN MY HEAD all through finals week and on into June, when I finally told Grandpa that I had to get out of town or explode.

He added creamer to his coffee. "So, no baseball this summer?"

"Not if I can help it."

"Do you suppose it'd help if I told you that game didn't make a hill of beans in the grand scheme of things? That the sun's gonna come up tomorrow?"

"No, that wouldn't help a damned bit."

"Well, I guess I won't tell you then. So, you want to get out of town. Can't see how that'd do any harm."

"You won't be lonely. You're over at Mrs. B.'s more than you're here."

"True. I'll miss you, though. Where do you want to go? LA?"

"No way. I saw an ad on the bulletin board at school for counselors at a camp up on the Michigan border."

"You'd probably enjoy that."

I shrugged. Right at the moment, I couldn't imagine enjoying anything beyond escape. "Mr. Franklin called the camp and gave them a lot of guff about how good I was with kids. They said they'd take me on. I can start next week, if I've got your permission."

"You've got it. Start packing, and I'll run you up on Saturday. Mind if I bring Ellen along?"

"No. That'd be okay."

I rode in the back, the tape of the game grinding away in my head, while Grandpa and Mrs. B. gabbed and cooed in the front. By the time they dropped me at Camp Forgotten Pine, I'd worked myself into one of the major bad moods of all time. But when I saw the blond girl behind the counter in the camp office, the game tape stopped with a *kachunk*. She smiled at me, and my knees went wobbly, like I'd tried to stand up too fast after sixteen innings behind the plate. "Hi," she said. "New counselor?"

"Uh, yeah. Neil Larsen from Shipley. They call me the Bull."

"I can believe that. You're big, aren't you?"

"I guess you could say that."

She shoved a form across the counter. "Well, at least I won't be stuck here all summer with a bunch of wimps. Fill this out while I get your handbook and stuff."

She started digging in a cabinet while I tried to fill out the form and ogle her at the same time. Lord, she had a body to die for. She plunked a pile of stuff on the counter. "Here's your cap, name tag, handbook, and three T-shirts, extra extra large. You'll be in Cabin Six with the eleven-year-olds. They're monsters, but it looks like you're big enough to handle them." She glanced at the form. "You missed a couple of spots."

"Oh, sorry."

"That's okay." She leaned an elbow on the counter and watched while I finished filling in the blanks. "So what brings you to Forgotten Pine?" she asked. "Can't be the money since we don't pay worth crap."

"Just wanted a change. Kind of sick of my hometown. How about you?"

"I'm Jenna Halvorson. My uncle runs the place. My parents send me here because they think it'll keep me out of trouble." She grinned at me. "They're wrong." The phone rang, and she reached for it. "We'll see you at supper, huh?"

"Uh, sure. Supper. I'll be there."

I dumped my stuff in Cabin Six, which was dusty and unswept, the mattresses folded double on the cots. I wandered down to the beach, figuring that sooner or later somebody'd tell me what to do. Behind me, a girl's voice yelled, "Hey, what do ya know, it *is* the Bull."

My head was still reeling from my encounter with Jenna and for a second I just stared at her. Who was this person? Bev Herkert. Good friend, good ballplayer, and not bad to look at if you liked big, muscular girls. But definitely not Jenna.

She gave me a hug. "I saw a Neil Larsen on the list and I thought it must be you. How ya doing, Bull?"

"Fine, Bev. How about you?" Fine? Hell, I hadn't been fine since the game.

"Better than ever. What are you doing here? I thought you lived to play baseball in the summer."

"Got kind of sick of it."

She stared up into my face, her brown eyes suddenly full of concern. "Oh, yeah. I read about the Caledonia game. I'm sorry. That must have been tough."

I nodded. "Yeah, it was. . . . So, what are you doing here?"

"Oh, I've been coming here for a couple of years. I teach first aid and help with the ten-year-olds."

"So you must know the ropes."

"Every one. And I can tie and untie them, too."

"Uh, nobody's told me much. What's the schedule?"

"Clean-up and orientation. The kids don't come until a week from tomorrow. This week we spruce up the camp and get some training from Mister Sam. That's Sam Halvorson, the camp director."

"Yeah, I met his niece."

She made a face. "The Princess Jenna. Well, she keeps things interesting around here. . . . Anyway, once we get the camp in shape, Mister Sam takes us into the Sylvania National Forest for three days of orientation. We practice paddling the canoes, setting up camp,

keeping out of the poison ivy. All the stuff we're supposed to teach the kiddies. Ever paddled a canoe?"

"A couple of times. I'm no expert."

"Then I'll have to make you one." She took my arm.
"Come on. Supper's not for a couple of hours yet."

We went canoeing, and it was good to be with her.
Because I liked Bev. As a friend, that is. Jenna might be
another matter.

The competition for Jenna was in full swing by the time
Bev and I got to the mess hall. "Hey, Bull," she yelled.
"Over here. I saved a place for you. You, too, Bev." She
looked at the guys at her table. "One of you guys move
over and make a place for Bev." Bev started to say something, but I was already moving toward the chair beside
Jenna.

Exactly why Jenna chose me that night, I'll never
know. But she did, focusing on me like there wasn't another guy in the room. And I returned the favor by shut-
ting out Bev. Jenna and I left the mess hall together after
Mister Sam finished his welcome speech. She showed
me the camp and then the nature trail beyond, and not
long after it started getting dark, she showed me some
other stuff, up close and personal. When we took a
breather, she ran a hand down my chest. "I like big
guys," she said. "And you're the biggest and best that's
come Jenna's way in quite a while."

"Just quite a while?"

"Well, maybe ever. We'll see."

They worked us hard until Wednesday afternoon, when Mister Sam gave us a few hours off to relax before the orientation trip into the Sylvania. I did my wash and then sat on the dock obsessing.

"Are you worrying about that dumb game again?" I turned to see Bev clomping onto the dock in her hiking boots.

I lied. "No, just enjoying the sunshine."

"The heck. I see you staring at your hands, and I know you're thinking about *the game*. It doesn't take Einstein to figure that one out." She sat down beside me and started unlacing her boots.

I shrugged. "Well, I guess it might have crossed my mind. Where's Jenna?"

"Stopped off to take a shower. That girl's got the worst body odor. Ever notice that?" She stuck her feet in the water and sighed. "God, have I been looking forward to this. Five miles is a long way to hike in this heat. . . . So, are you looking forward to tomorrow? The orientation trip is usually kind of fun."

"It'll beat brushing."

"I'll bet. Cleaning cabins wasn't much fun, either, but everything looks pretty good now."

"Yeah, it does. We've done a lot."

"Most of us. Jenna got to sit in the office again today."

"Privilege of being the owner's niece."

She grunted sourly. "I guess . . ." She swirled the water with her toes and contemplated the opposite shore of the lake. "Want to skip supper?" she asked. "We could take one of the canoes over to the landing and walk into town. They've got good burgers at Molly's, and it'll be our last chance to get away for a couple of weeks."

I hesitated. "Sorry, but I've got some other plans."

She sighed. "Okay. Forget I asked." She dried her feet with a sock and pulled on her boots. "I've gotta get some fresh socks before the dinner bell."

"Thanks anyway, Bev. Another time, huh?"

"Sure," she said, and started up the dock toward the cabins.

The dinner bell clanged a few minutes later, interrupting my thoughts before I could get heavy into viewing the game tape again. I levered myself up and started for the mess hall to meet Jenna.

Jenna and I had already planned to skip supper for burgers at Molly's and a stopover at an island on our return trip. I conjured some X-rated fantasies while I waited for her behind the mess hall. She slammed out of the camp office and came striding angrily across the clearing. "What's the matter?" I asked.

"Uncle Sam says I've got to call my mother after supper! And then he wants me to staple some stupid handbooks for tomorrow. It'll take me all evening."

My fantasies started imploding. "Oh . . . Well, maybe I could help you. Then we —"

She glared at me. "Don't be stupid, Bull. The idea is to keep Jenna from having a good time. And that means under guard."

Mister Sam came out of the office, putting his cap on over his balding head. He frowned at us. She glared at him, spun on her heel, and marched into the mess hall. I followed, trying to look small. A tough trick for the Bull.

"Got everything?" Bev asked as I heaved my pack into the back of one of the trucks.

"Everything on the list."

"Well, if Jenna typed it, she probably left off half the stuff. But don't worry, we're not going to the arctic or anything."

I looked out across the lake, shining blue under a clear sky. "Why don't we leave from here, instead of riding the trucks for an hour?"

"This lake is kid stuff. Back in the Sylvania, you get the real wilderness experience." She looked toward the office, where Jenna was arguing with Mister Sam. He shook his head, and Jenna stomped her foot, grabbed her pack, and headed for the landing. "Doesn't look like the Princess Jenna wants the real wilderness experience," Bev said. "What do you see in her, anyway?"

"Come on, Bev. You know that's not fair."

"No, really. I swear I'm not jealous. I'm just curious." Jenna tried to swing her pack into one of the trucks but didn't put enough muscle into it. She lost her grip, and it tumbled to the ground. She kicked it. "Well," Bev said, "better go help her before she starts crying."

I boosted Jenna's pack into the truck. She grouched a thank you, climbed in, and commenced to pout. We bounced along for twenty miles, the canoe trailer rattling behind. The road dead-ended at a small grassy bay on a big lake, where Mister Sam had said: "We'll put civilization behind us." (A statement that had spawned a fair number of cracks about opportunities for uncivilized behavior.)

"This must be the place," I said.

Jenna glared at the landing. "Yeah, this is the place, all right."

"Why are you so ornery?"

"Because I've done this trip about ten times. I don't want to do it again."

"But I'm along this time."

She snorted. "Don't get your hopes up, boy. Uncle Sam has picked you out, and he's going to watch us like a hawk. Well, we'll just see about that."

I didn't have any feelings about Mister Sam one way or the other, but I didn't want to cross him and get my butt fired. "Maybe we ought to play it cool."

She glared at me. "You think so, huh?"

"Well, what else can we —"

"Plenty," she snapped, and climbed out of the truck without another word.

We set about getting the canoes off the trailers and loading them at the lakeside. "Jenna," Mister Sam called, "you take stern in number eight."

"Uncle Sam! I want to ride with Bull."

"Uh-uh. You've got more experience than most of these kids. You take a stern."

She stomped her foot (again), hefted her pack, and tromped over to number eight. Ed Miller hurried to grab the bow position, narrowly beating out Dave Blackaby. A couple of canoes away, Bev and a tall athletic girl — Sarah somebody — started giggling. Dave drifted over to my canoe. "I guess you're stuck with me," he said.

"I guess," I said. "Want the stern?"

"Nah, you take it. This is all pretty new to me."

We shoved off, Mister Sam leading the way. Dave and I found the rhythm quickly, and we were soon up toward the front of the pack of nine canoes. Bev and Sarah swung in alongside. "How you guys doing?" Bev called.

"Fine," I said. "How far to the first portage?"

"Couple of miles. Better start reading your map. You'll need to know how next week."

I pulled out the copy of the map we'd been given and studied it. "Leave that until later," Dave groused. "We go all cockeyed when you stop paddling."

We fell into a rough line as we skirted the eastern shore of the lake. The pines and hardwoods grew down to the shoreline, their reflection reaching out across the water so that we seemed to paddle as much in forest as lake. But despite all the beauty to distract me, the tape of the game started playing in my head again. Damn it, I'd seen Phuong's pitch clearly, all the way past Gary Melcher's flailing bat and straight into my mitt. How the hell had I missed it?

The first portage produced a lot of flailing around, but we finally managed to get the canoes and the gear lugged across the three hundred yards to the next lake. The second portage went better, but some of the kids were really dragging by the time we reached the campsite on the far side of the third lake. I couldn't believe how much my shoulders ached, and I'd been playing ball all spring.

Mister Sam parceled out the jobs. Bev and Sarah got cooking duty, while Dave and I got stuck setting up tents (verifying the usual sexist policies of Forgotten Pine). Jenna and Ed disappeared into the woods to gather firewood. They were gone a long time, and when they came back, Ed was looking just a little too happy. I gave Jenna a hard look, but she ignored me. I caught Bev watching me. I glared at her. She gave a tiny shrug and went back to tending her frying pan.

When supper was over and the dishes washed, Mister Sam lectured on the big four dangers of camping: fire, water, sharp instruments, and ticks. He had some pretty hair-raising stories about flaming, drowned, maimed, and bitten kiddies — none from Camp Forgotten Pine, of course. "How about bears, wolves, and that sort of stuff?" Sarah asked.

"Don't worry about them. You'll never see the few wolves still around, and the bears won't give you any trouble as long as you hang your food packs like I showed you. Jenna, you tell 'em what happened last year when your crew forgot to hang a food pack. . . .

Where's Jenna?" We looked around. Where was Ed? Mister Sam spotted me and glared. I shrugged.

"We're over here, Uncle Sam." Jenna led Ed back into the clearing. She dropped an armful of wood by the fire. "Just getting some bigger pieces." Ed nodded in agreement. He looked happier than ever.

"Well, stay close. You need to hear this just like everybody else."

"Sure, Uncle Sam." She gave him her biggest smile and went to sit near Ed. There were a few whispers behind me, and I felt my face flush.

Mister Sam went on lecturing for another half hour and then gave us a break. "Come on, Ed," Jenna said. "We need more firewood." I watched them go. To hell with it.

Mister Sam got out an ax and started splitting some of the bigger logs. I leaned back, watching the rise and fall of the ax in the firelight. Mad as I was at Jenna, my eyelids started growing heavy. And, of course, the tape of the game started rolling in my head again. Sign down, Phuong nodding and then checking Lutz at third. Then his arm coming up over the top, the ball flashing in the instant before it left his —

It happened so fast that for a second I couldn't believe it had happened at all. Mister Sam brought the ax down on a piece of pine, the blade glancing off a knot and slicing into his foot. He dropped the ax and stumbled back, blood spouting from his boot. I moved like I was lunging after a wild pitch and caught him as he started to fall.

Somebody was beside me, her fingers tearing at the laces of Mister Sam's boot. Bev. "He hit an artery," she snapped. "We've got to get pressure on it or he's going to bleed to death." She got her hand under the tongue of his boot and pressed, the gout of blood bubbling through her fingers. "Somebody give me a clean rag or a T-shirt or something," she shouted. "And a flash-light."

Mister Sam tried to sit up. "Let me see," he said, his voice more angry than scared.

"Mister Sam, you just lie down," Bev said. "I don't want you losing any more blood than you have to."

He started to protest, but I said, "Do what she says, Mister Sam. She's the first-aid expert."

"Nice of you to remember," she said. Somebody brought the lantern over. She took a breath. "Okay, help me get his boot off."

I took the heel and toe and slid it off as gently as I could. The ax blade had cut deep, severing muscle and bone from the top of his foot to the middle of his toes. Behind me, I heard a couple of kids groan and run for the woods to puke. Somebody handed Bev a folded T-shirt, and she pressed it over the gaping wound.

"Oh, my God. What happened?" Jenna threw herself down beside us and started babbling: "It's okay, Uncle Sam. You're going to be okay. Just be calm. I'm right —"

"Jenna, go dunk your head in the lake," Bev said. "We're busy here."

"You can't talk to me like that, you dumb cow."

"Jenna!" Mister Sam snapped. "Get control of yourself and let the people with some brains take care of things."

"Uncle Sam!"

"You," he pointed at Ed. "Get her away from here until she calms down." Ed, who was looking a bit green, seemed only too happy to oblige.

Sarah had found the first-aid kit. Bev replaced the bloody T-shirt with a pressure bandage and used the scissors to cut Mister Sam's pants to the knee. "Mister Sam," she said, "do you want me to put on a tourniquet?"

"Yes, but don't tighten it. I'll take care of that. Okay, there's a ranger station on Big Pike, two lakes over. That's the closest road access. We'll take two canoes. Bev, you're in charge. I trust you to read a map. Where's Monty?"

Monty Schneider, a tall, quiet kid who'd been a counselor for a couple of years, stepped up. "Here, boss."

"You're in charge here. Break camp in the morning . . ."

While he gave Monty instructions, Bev and I looked at each other. Her face was splattered with blood and her hands looked like she'd butchered a pig. I looked down at my own bloody hands and acid shot into my throat. I swallowed. "I'll come," I said. "That's if you want —"

"Don't be stupid," she said. "Of course, I want you." She looked up at the circle of kids. "Bull and I'll take Mister Sam in one canoe. Who wants to take the other?"

"I'll go," Dave said. "As long as somebody else paddles stern."

"I know how to paddle stern," Sarah said.

Bev took a deep breath. "Okay, let's do it."

A half dozen kids helped carry Mister Sam down to the canoes. Jenna ran up and started climbing into Dave and Sarah's. I reached for her shoulder. "You'd be extra baggage, Jenna. Stay here and help Monty."

"You can't order me around!"

"Oh, yeah? Try me, and we'll see how well you can swim."

She spun away and started climbing into the canoe again. I grabbed her around the waist and carried her kicking up the bank. "Here, Ed. She's yours and welcome to her. Now keep her here, or I'll throw you both in." I dumped her in his arms.

"Build up the fire," Bev yelled. "I'll need to sight on it."

A steady drizzle started falling before we were halfway across the lake. Bev peered ahead, turning now and again to take a bearing on the fire. Mister Sam groaned, shifting the pressure on the tourniquet. "A little to your left, Bev," he said. "Beyond that little island."

I could just make out the dark shape of the island through the drizzle. Good thing I wasn't in charge or we'd be lost already. We left the island behind, paddling across a wide stretch of open water as the fire shrank to a distant glimmer. "Mister Sam," Bev said, a quiver slipping into her voice, "I don't know where the portage is. North or south from here?"

"North." His voice had a fuzzy edge.

We swung in close to the shore, following Dave and Sarah as they swept the trees with a big flashlight. "Over there," Sarah yelled. "We can see the sign."

"Thank God," Bev breathed.

When our canoe ground on the shore, I scrambled out, the water running in over the top of my boots. I helped Bev out and together we pulled the bow onto the beach. Dave and I reached in, got our arms under Mister Sam and lifted. "God, he's heavy," Dave panted.

"Wait until you hit forty, son," Mister Sam gritted through the pain. "It'll happen to you, too."

Bev came to help, and the three of us managed to carry him to the head of the narrow trail disappearing into the woods. "Let me try to walk," he said.

"Not on your life," Bev said. "And I'm not fooling."

"This isn't working," I said. "Get him on my back."

They hoisted him so I could carry him piggyback, his arms around my neck. "I'll keep a hand on his back," Bev said.

"I can hold on," Mister Sam said. "Go back for a canoe."

Sarah went ahead with the flashlight, and I followed, the weight of Mister Sam growing heavier by the step. "Are you okay?" Sarah called back. "Need to rest?"

"No, keep going," I panted, knowing that if I stopped it'd be twice as hard to start again. Ahead through the trees, I could see the faint reflection of the next lake. I felt a sticky warmth on my right thigh. Blood. Lots of it. Mister Sam's arms started loosening around my neck. "Sarah!" I shouted, and just managed to grab one of his arms as he started sliding off my back. She came running, got her arms around him, and we managed to ease him down.

"He's fainted," she said.

"Get Bev. Hurry."

"Bev!" she shouted, and ran down the trail. I felt for the bandage, found the warm wetness of it, and pressed down hard, my other hand trying to find the tourniquet. I was frightened of twisting it too tight, but the blood was coming fast, bubbling from under the bandage. "Mister Sam! Wake up. I need your help, damn it."

Bev came pounding up. She knelt. "Hold the flashlight. . . . " She was breathing hard and her hands shook. "Steady, girl," she muttered, and her hands became sure. "This is bad, Bull. I can slow it down, but I can't get it stopped."

We heard Dave and Sarah coming with a canoe. "Let's get him to the landing before they run over us," I said.

"Right . . . Okay, ready?"

"Ready." We lifted him between us and stumbled toward the lake.

Dave and Sarah dumped the canoe on the shore.

"Guys," Bev said, "we've got to move faster. We'll start, you get the other canoe and try to catch up." She studied the map and then the dim outline of the lake through the drizzle. "Crap, I can't see anything. I'm going to have to go by compass alone. Okay, let's get him in the canoe."

We paddled out into the lake. "We'll see you at the next portage," Sarah shouted.

"Hurry. We're going to need your help," Bev called.

We bent to the paddles, pushing hard for the shadowy outline of the far shore. I timed my strokes to hers, throwing in an occasional J-stroke to keep us straight. Despite the coolness of the drizzle, I could feel the sweat running down my back, and with it came the good, hot-muscle feeling I got behind the plate. Game time.

In the center of the canoe, Mister Sam muttered something, tried to sit up, and slumped back. "Let's pick it up," Bev said.

"Bring it on," I growled.

"You're doing fine, Bull. Perfect."

"So are you. You're really something."

She snorted. "Don't start sweet-talking me. You had your chance." She hit her stroke and the canoe shot ahead.

I don't know how she did it in the darkness and the rain, but after two more checks of the compass, she turned the big flashlight on the shore and said, "There. Up the shore to the left."

I squinted and made out the reflection of the portage sign in the wavering light of the flashlight. "Got it."

On shore, I swung Mister Sam up into a fireman's carry. "Just grab the paddles and lead the way."

The rain came rustling through the leaves as I followed Bev through the dark corridor of trees. For a while, the good heat carried me along, but his weight bore down on me until my shoulders and neck cramped and my legs started going rubber. Don't stop. Stop, and you're finished.

I tried counting my steps, but that only made things worse. In desperation, I switched on the tape of the game. I'd watch the final inning. Get mad at myself. March because the anger would make me forget everything else. But the tape stuttered, refusing to settle into play. Somewhere, way back when, I'd played a game, but I couldn't recall the details anymore as I trudged through the hunching shadows with Mister Sam's weight crushing me into the earth.

Bev was beside me, her arm around my waist. "What?" I panted.

"You were laughing. Or crying, maybe."

"It's nothing. Keep going."

"Only a little farther."

"I know. I can see it. It shines."

"Bull!"

"No, look. I tell you, it shines."

She turned to look and saw, as I had seen, the moon

breaking through the clouds to shine silver on the lake. I staggered the last few dozen yards to the water's edge and together we eased Mister Sam down by the lapping waves. I stood, wobbling under the sudden lightness of him not being there, and stared out along the silver track of the moon. God, it was beautiful.

"We've got to go back for the canoe," Bev said. "Do you think he'll be all right for a few minutes?"

"You stay with him. I'll get it."

She took a ragged breath. "Bull, we can't wait for Dave and Sarah. They might have gotten lost, and we don't have a lot of time. Not the way he's bleeding."

Time no longer seemed real as I crossed the portage trail. I knew I was hurrying by the sound of my boots on the wet earth, but every chirp, every rustle in the woods came to me as clearly as if I'd been strolling along through the night without a care in the world. At the shore, I searched the lake, hoping for the glimmer of Sarah's flashlight, but saw nothing but emptiness on the water.

I went to the canoe. I could make this carry, could make it because I was beyond fatigue and fear now. Weight, muscle, and motion. Simple things. I grasped the center thwart, made the lift, and started up the trail, minding my balance, cushioning the jolts of the rocks and roots with my knees, eating the distance.

Waiting in the darkness with Mister Sam, Bev too had gone beyond something. I could hear it in her voice, although all she said was: "He's unconscious. We've got to move."

I scooped him up and laid him as gently as I could in the canoe. Then we were on the water again, the rhythm coming easily, our paddles leaving swirls of reflected moonlight behind us. Far off across the water a loon called, its cry unearthly, as the clouds frayed into tatters, letting the stars shine through.

We rounded an island and saw the light of the ranger station at the end of a cove. We started yelling when we were still a couple of hundred yards from shore, and the house lights came on. The ranger came out on the porch, and Bev shouted the story across the water.

The second we bumped against the dock, everything was out of our control. The ranger and his wife bundled Mister Sam into the back of a 4×4 truck, the ranger scrambling in with a first-aid kit. The ranger's wife clambered into the driver's seat. "We called the hospital," she shouted. "The ambulance will meet us on the way."

"Do you think he'll be all right?" Bev asked.

"If we hurry. Don't worry. You kids did just fine. Go into the house and get some breakfast."

We looked at each other. "If it's all the same," Bev said, "I think we'll head back. We left a couple of friends out there."

"Well, make some sandwiches to take along, then. We'll be in touch with the camp." The engine roared, and they were off.

Suddenly, there didn't seem much to do. We found the kitchen, helped ourselves to bread, peanut butter, and a couple of cans of pop.

We paddled out beyond the island in the early light, then shipped our paddles and dug into the sandwiches. A breeze rocked the canoe, pushing us gently east toward the sunrise. Far across the water, I caught a glint of silver. "There's the other canoe," I said. "They found the portage after all. I suppose we ought to go tell them that they don't have to hurry."

"I think they've figured that out. Looks like they're taking it easy."

"I guess you're right," I said. "I could use another sandwich, anyway."

We sat for a while longer, waiting for the sun as the breeze ruffled the water all the way to the far green shore. Experimentally, I pushed the play button on my mental VCR, but the tape only chattered, its broken ends snapping around the heads. Well, I'd mend it someday when I had the time.

The sun crested the trees, unrolling a warm light across the water. Bev turned in the bow seat to smile at me. I grinned at her. "How you doin', sunshine?"

She stuck her tongue out at me. "Don't call me nicknames. I happen to like my name."

"Okay. And maybe you ought to call me Neil. I think I'm going to give up being the Bull for a while."

"Oh? Do you think Jenna will approve?"

"Jenna who?" I said.

Bev and I never said "I love you" that summer. Perhaps we didn't have to, or perhaps it wasn't quite what we felt for each other. But we did feel very good together. Forgotten Pine didn't give a lot of time off, but we managed to schedule the ten- and eleven-year-olds together for the same activity a lot of the time. We took them canoeing and swimming, played volleyball and softball, and now and then just let them run around like the little animals they were. I liked them and I liked the work.

Jenna ignored me for a few days and then decided to be polite. With Mister Sam laid up, she had to do more of the work, and I think that did her good. I even started to like her, which — come to think of it — I really hadn't before.

But Bev . . . Well, that was liking and something. And I knew that I ought to get around to sorting that out one of these days.

I was just about to let my eleven-year-olds go into the water when Sarah yelled, "Hey, Bull. You've got a phone call up at the office."

"I've got kids here. Who is it?"

"They didn't say. Go ahead, I'll cover for you."

I told her thanks and jogged up to the office. Jenna was frowning at a bill. She waved toward the phone lying on Mister Sam's desk. I picked it up and said hello.

"Bull, it's me."

"Hey, Jeff. How you doin'?"

"I'm okay. How're things up there?"

"Great. I'm really enjoying it. You winning some games?"

"Oh, yeah. We're winning a couple here and there. . . . Uh, Bull, I've got some bad news."

I felt my stomach lurch. "Is it my grandpa? Is he okay?"

"Yeah, he's fine. Sitting right here. It's Billy. He was killed last night."

I slumped back against the desk. "Oh, God. How?"

"Car accident. He hit the bridge abutment out where old eighty-seven crosses the river. Probably driving drunk. He'd been doing that a lot lately. All summer, really. Sandi couldn't handle it anymore, and they broke up about three weeks ago. After that, he really lost it. I tried to talk to him, but, shit, he wouldn't listen to anybody anymore."

There was a long pause. Finally, I managed to ask, "Have you talked to Sandi?"

"No, but I talked to her dad. He said she's handling things. . . . She'll be okay, Bull. She always is. You know that."

Yeah, I knew that. "When's the funeral?"

"Day after tomorrow."

"Shit, I'm supposed to be out in the Sylvania on a trip."

"Your granddad says nobody's going to think any worse of you if you don't make it."

"Maybe I'd better talk to him."

"Yeah, maybe you'd better. . . . But, Bull, I'm sorry. I —" Suddenly his control broke and he was crying. "I shouldn't have let this happen! I should have stopped him."

I was crying, too, but I managed to get it out. "Jeff, it's

214

not your fault. It was Billy, man. Crazy Billy and his crazy, screwed-up family."

"I know, but . . . Oh, hell." I heard the receiver clatter on the table.

A moment later, Grandpa came on the line. "I'm sorry, Grandson. Jeff's taking this pretty hard."

"Is he still there?"

"He went out back."

"Grandpa, talk to him, huh? Tell him that it's not his fault. Jeff always thought he should take care of all of us. But Billy —"

"I know. I'll talk to him."

For a long minute, neither of us spoke. Finally, I said, "Grandpa, I've gotta be by myself for a little while. I'll call you tonight, huh?"

"Okay. But, Neil, I'm awfully sorry about Billy. The poor kid really had it rough."

When I hung up the phone, Jenna was staring at me, her mouth hanging a little open. Then she got up and very deliberately carried a box of tissues over to me. I took some. "What happened?" she asked in a small voice.

"A friend got killed in a car accident. A real mixed-up —" I couldn't finish.

She put her arms around me. "I'm sorry."

We must have looked pretty stupid: me crying and this girl about a foot shorter and half my size hugging me and patting me on the back. But I appreciated it.

That evening I tried to explain Billy to Bev. But I couldn't. Not really, because you had to have known him, like only those of us who'd grown up with him really could. And although Bev said all the right things, they didn't really help, because I knew that when Billy'd needed me in the last year, I'd turned my back — and that was something I'd have to bear knowing for the rest of my life.

The first letter from Sandi came a few days later, as we were getting ready for the final week with the kids. She didn't say a lot important until the end. Instead, she rambled on about her summer job teaching tennis at the Y, about how she'd been trying to teach herself Spanish, and about shopping for a puppy for her little sister's birthday. But on the last page, she wrote:

> *I guess Jeff told you that I broke up with Billy a couple of weeks before the accident. Billy was so drunk that night that I was afraid he was going to kill us both. And that's when I told him I couldn't see him anymore. He told me he didn't care and I guess maybe he didn't. He was a sweet guy and I loved him and tried to give him some help. But in the end, I don't think that was what he really wanted.*
>
> *Hope you're having a good time.*
>
> *Love,*
> *Sandi*

Bev and I didn't get much time together that last week, so there was a lot still unsaid when her dad came to pick her up on Saturday. I helped her carry her stuff

216

to the car. A lot of little kids were hanging around, waiting for their parents, and as usual, a lot of them found an excuse to trail after me.

"You sure are the favorite," Bev said.

"I thought they were following you."

"Nope, the kiddies love their Bull. Hang on him, beat on him, tickle him. Nothing fazes him."

"Well, they are cute. . . . I wish you could stick around for the closing up."

"Oh, I've got to make this family reunion. I haven't seen some of my cousins in a couple of years. Besides, closing up is just a lot of nasty, dirty work. I might ruin my nails."

"You sound like Jenna."

"Careful, boy. Those are pretty close to fighting words."

"Anytime. I always enjoy a good tussle with you."

"I know the kind of tussle you enjoy." We set her cardboard boxes on a picnic table by the parking lot, and she shooed away our entourage of little kids. "Go on. Get out of here. Beat it." They retreated a few feet, giggling. She turned to face me. "So I guess this is the hard part," she said.

"I guess . . . I'll miss you. A whole lot."

"Me, too." She stepped into my arms, her face up to mine.

"Ooooohhh," all the kids went as we kissed.

She stepped back, trying to smile, her eyes glistening. "I'll write you if you write me."

217

"I will," I said.

She turned away quickly. "Here," she said, shoving the box I'd been carrying at the biggest kid. "Carry this. The rest of you, keep him here."

The kid followed Bev across the lot as the others swirled in around me, giggling and grabbing on to me.

If I hadn't been such a stupid jerk, I would have kept my promise. But by that time, I'd had a second letter from Sandi, and although it hadn't said even as much as the first, the last two words were the same. And for all that Bev had meant to me, those two lousy words — "Love, Sandi" — still meant more.

FALL –
SENIOR YEAR

THE MINUTE I GOT IN THE CAR with Grandpa
and Mrs. B., I could tell that his "caterwauling" days
were over for good. They were comfortable together —
agreed and settled in. And that was fine, of course, except that it left me out. I gave them a summary of the
last couple of weeks at camp, which took about a
minute and a half, and they brought me up on the news
from home, which wasn't much except for the painful
business of Billy's funeral.

"Your mother called last night," Grandpa said. "She
wants us to fly out to Colorado Springs. She has a couple of days' work there, and then she thought we could
drive down to the Grand Canyon."

"What'd you tell her?"

"Oh, I said that you might have some time in your

219

schedule but that I was kind of booked up." He grinned at Mrs. B.

I hadn't missed Shipley at all, and the more I thought about it, the more I liked the idea of seeing the Grand Canyon. But whatever Mom was doing in Colorado Springs suddenly needed a week and the trip never came off. "I'm sorry, Neil," she said on the phone.

"That's okay, Mom. We'll do it another time."

"I just get so busy, sometimes. We've brought in two new associates in the last year, but there are still things that Norma and I just can't trust to anybody else. This is one of them."

"I understand."

"Thank you, dear. I've penciled in ten days at Christmas. We'll have fun, then."

"Sure, Mom."

I really hadn't focused on the reality that I was going to be a senior, so it was a shock to find Jeff sorting through college brochures when I dropped by his house. "Did you send for all of these?"

"No, they sent them to me."

"I had a few waiting when I got home, but not like this."

He shrugged. "Well, most of them don't count for much. Places that cost too much or don't have much of a program."

"As in baseball program."

"What else?"

"Every one of these places wants you to play ball?"

"Far as I can tell. And speaking of ball . . ." He glanced at his watch. "I was going to get together with some of the guys at three."

"Hey, that'd be good. I haven't played all summer."

He looked at me. "Yeah, I know. . . . So, did you bring a glove?"

"Didn't think to. I'll run home and get one."

Sandi came over the next evening, and we sat together on the front steps until dark. I wanted to reach out for her, but I didn't dare. Not yet. So, I just listened while she talked for a long time about Billy in an odd, flat voice that didn't sound anything like the Sandi I knew. When at last she stood, I started to get up, but she put her hands on my shoulders. "I'm okay walking by myself. I'll see you soon." She hesitated, and then leaned forward to kiss me, her lips lingering experimentally on mine. But when I tried to put an arm around her, she broke off the kiss. "Wait," she said.

Over the summer, they'd built a new wing onto the high school, and we reopened in the fall as a four-year school. The freshmen seemed incredibly young. And squirrelly. "Were we that bad?" I yelled to Phuong over the din in the hall.

"Some of us. Not me."

"Uh-huh. And what are you implying, my slant-eyed friend?"

"Nothing much. By the way, in Vietnam they call Caucasians round-eyes. Bet you didn't know that."

"No, I didn't. How was the trip, anyway?"

"Real good. My dad had some real positive meetings with government officials. By next summer, everything should be go for the clinic."

"He's not going to move back there, is he?"

"No, that's never been the plan. He'll just help get everything up and running, then he'll come back here to stay current in his field. He'll fly over a couple of times a year to teach a workshop, and he'll consult by fax the rest of the time."

"Hope you didn't spend all your time sitting in meetings."

"No, I got out and around quite a bit. Shot about a bezillion pictures." We dodged half a dozen amuck freshmen. "You know," he said, "I figured it out, and with this big freshman class, seniors make up less than a fifth of the school population."

"Yeah, and what's more, nobody's paying any attention to us. I thought we were supposed to be the big news this year."

"No, we're the old news. This school belongs to the freshmen now. They're the first class that'll go all the way through."

"Still pisses me off. No respect."

"Ah, who's got time to worry about that? We've got the future to think about."

And that's what all the other seniors seemed to be doing, all right. But somehow, I'd bogged down, caught back at the end of the throng, still trying to figure out the present.

I called Sandi, and after a long hesitation, she said, "Sure, I'll go out with you Saturday."

I could hardly believe it. "Where do you want to go?"

"The movies, I guess. I'm kind of fond of escaping reality these days."

Jeff tossed his towel over the locker door and started dressing. "So, you finally talked her into it?"

"Yeah. See anything wrong with that?"

"Not if it's what you want."

He pulled a T-shirt over his head, and I noticed how it stretched tight over his chest. "You put on some muscle over the summer."

"Four pounds. I'm going to add six more by opening day. Looks like you put on a few pounds, too."

I looked down at my stomach, which did have a bit of a bulge to it. "A couple, I guess. They fed us pretty good up there. Don't worry, I've got it under control."

"Good, because you don't need anything more slowing you down."

"So you've been telling me for about ten years."

"About. So you gonna do some training this winter?"

223

"Sure. You and me, just like always."

"Well, maybe not quite. I've signed up most of the guys I figure to be playing a lot next spring. Soon as football and cross-country are over, we're going to play some basketball. Greg's getting the juniors on one intramural team, I'm getting the seniors on another. Between games, we'll work on the weights and a few drills. Then after Christmas, we'll start doing some hitting."

"You get the pitchers lined up, too?"

"All of 'em except Phuong. He says he's too busy."

"Just like old times."

"Well, we can't afford any more old times. We've got one shot and you can bet Caledonia's gonna be tougher than ever. They lost fewer starters and their new guys are at least as good as ours. Probably better. Remember that McHugh kid? Well, I don't think Lord Parkenham is ever going to be in his class, but he'd better narrow the gap some or we're gonna be sucking tailpipe."

God, it'd been a long time since I'd thought about any of this. I shrugged. "Well, Ed's got some growing to do, but I think he'll be okay."

"Good. But will you talk to Phuong? If he doesn't want to play basketball, fine. But he needs to do some training just like the rest of us."

I didn't make talking to Phuong a high priority, since I was concentrating on getting a good start in my classes. For a decent high school catcher with more than average power but with . . . well, something less than average speed, grades might make the difference between getting in or just missing a major college program. And I wanted a big one: Arizona State, New Mexico, USC, or one of the few others that regularly sent players on to the big leagues.

Finally, after Jeff nagged me for about the fourth time, I talked to Phuong. He smiled. "Just like old times."

"That's what I told Jeff."

"I'm sorry, Bull, but I just don't have time. Not this winter."

I shrugged. "Hey, I'm not worried. Give you and me a week together in the spring, and we'll be ready to go."

He hesitated. "Yeah, sure. A week and no problem."

"The scouts are going to be all over you this season. Even more than Jeff. Good pitchers are the hottest item going."

He laughed. "I'm not worried about them. Only Jeff's *got* to play ball."

"And me."

He smiled. "Sure. And you, too. But not me. At least not until spring."

I answered Bev's first two or three letters, although I had a hard time doing it. Damn, I liked her. I'd never felt more at ease with a girl. But now that Sandi and I were together — or getting that way — I really ought to tell Bev: "Gee, thanks for the good times, but save your time and postage." But I didn't have the guts.

Early in October, she sent a card inviting me for

the weekend of the Shipley-McArthur football game: "Mom said it's okay, and everybody'd love to see you. Especially this body." As always, she put her drawing of a fluffy black cat on the bottom of the card with a bubble saying, "Love ya."

So, I had to tell her. I sat at my desk for a long time, making one false start after another. Finally, I just told the truth. And that was hard, because the more I thought about it, the more I was sure that at least for a while I had loved Bev. And that I should have said so.

Her reply came a few days later: a sheet bare except for the drawing of the cat and the one word, "Oh."

Sandi let me kiss her, but that was all. And even after nearly three months together, her kiss still seemed experimental, lingering not because she seemed to enjoy it but because it still seemed odd to her that we were kissing at all. Then she'd push me gently but firmly away. "Wait. I'm still thinking."

"About what?"

"I'm not sure. I'm not sure about anything."

"You can be sure about me."

She studied. "That much I know. But do I want to be?"

"You can't go wrong."

"Maybe not." She kissed me again, giving in this time just a little.

* * *

Phuong asked me to meet him at Jeff's. "What's up?" I asked.

"Jeff keeps nagging me about training with the rest of you guys, and I guess I should explain some things."

"It's no big deal as far as I'm concerned. Just tell Jeff you'll be ready come the season and to leave you alone for now."

"It's a little more complicated than that. I'll explain everything when we get there."

I drove the six blocks to Jeff's in Grandpa's fishing car, which had pretty much become my vehicle for the winter. Up ahead, I saw Phuong, his shoulders hunched against a December wind blowing sharp flurries of snow out of the northwest. I beeped the horn and pulled to the curb beside him.

He climbed in. "Thanks. It's cold out there." He brushed snowflakes from a thick photo album.

"What've you got there?" I asked.

"Pictures."

"Of what?"

"You'll see."

In Jeff's kitchen, Phuong showed us page after page of pictures from Vietnam. A lot of them were of sick people being treated in hospitals that looked clean enough but short on equipment and lighting. Then came pictures of American clinics in Madison, Seattle, and good old Shipley. Finally, Phuong flipped through page after page of diagrams and floor plans. "So," he said, "that's the kind of place we're going to build in Phu Loc."

Jeff, who'd been fighting to look interested, said, "That's great, Phuong. What kind of clinic did you call it?"

"Gastroenterology. That's my dad's specialty, and this will be the first clinic of its type in that part of the country. And they need one a lot. Intestinal tract infections really play hell with people there."

"Did you do this whole album?" I asked.

"Uh-huh. Papa didn't have time, so I did it. It's been real useful, both over there and back here."

"You ought to be proud," I said. "It's really something."

"So," Jeff said, "next summer you'll be going over to help build the clinic, huh?"

Phuong shook his head. "Not next summer. This winter. The government changed plans, and now we're going to start building in February. So, that's where I'm going to be."

"For how long?" I asked.

"July or August."

"But graduation —"

"I have enough credits to graduate in January, and I've already been accepted at the University of Chicago. I got the letter last week."

Jeff was staring at the tabletop. Now he raised his eyes. "So, you're just going to say to hell with us and jump right into college ball?"

Phuong shook his head. "No, the University of Chicago doesn't have a baseball team. And I wouldn't try out even if they did. It takes a long time to become a doctor, and I don't want to make it any longer than I have to." He closed the album. "Because, you see, there are some things that really need doing. Like this."

Jeff's voice was bitter. "You're letting a lot of people down, Phuong. A lot of guys busted their tails to get you all those wins in the last couple of years. And now you're walking out on them."

If anything, I felt worse than he did, but I said, "Jeff, don't —"

"No, I need to say this. And Phuong, don't you write me off as some insensitive jock who doesn't care about helping sick people. Because I know that's important. But I also know it's important to stick with the team, to finish what we started together a long damn time ago. And you know it, too."

Phuong didn't argue. He took something out of his coat pocket and held it out: a baseball, scuffed brown in spots, the scrawled signatures on it already fading. "From the time we beat Caledonia way back in summer league," he said. "The one time we ever did it." Very carefully, he set it on the table. "It's been sitting on a shelf in my bedroom ever since, and it's meant a lot to me. Now one of you guys should have it. For luck."

He got up quickly, pulled on his coat, and started for the door. "Baseball never really meant that much to you, did it, Phuong?" Jeff asked.

He turned. "Not the game. But you guys did. A lot."

* * *

At first, I didn't understand. "Are you sick?"

"No, I just can't go out with you Saturday," Sandi said.

"Why? Do your parents have something planned?"

"No, Bull. Another guy called me, and I'm going out with him."

"Hey, wait a —"

"No, you wait! Don't you try to own me. That was Billy's problem. He thought he owned me and that he had the right to drag me down with him. But he didn't own me and you don't, either. Which means I will go out with anybody I darn well please!"

I didn't say anything, couldn't say anything.

She was breathing hard, which made her voice even harsher when she said, "And I do love you, Bull. But you've got to keep your distance until I tell you it's okay to come closer. Now, I'll see you Monday."

On Monday, she took my arm in the hall outside the trigonometry room and stood on tiptoes to kiss me. "I told you I'd see you on Monday. You look good."

What I wanted to ask was: "How was your date Saturday, and what's the guy's name so I can kill him?" But I couldn't, of course, and all I could think of to say was: "Uh, Swenson's giving back tests. How do think you did?"

She raised her eyebrows. "An A. I always get A's, remember. That's because I'm smart, not just cute."

"Oh, yeah," I said. "I forgot."

She did get an A, of course. I did, too, although I wasn't as smart as she was. Not even close.

The ten days Mom had penciled in at Christmas shrank to a long weekend. She explained to Grandpa, Mrs. B., and me at Christmas dinner. "It's just that we're right at the critical stage right now. If we don't make the deal this next week, we may never make it."

"But if you sell," I said, "you won't own your own firm anymore." (Which was, of course, pretty damned obvious.)

"No, but we'll be vice presidents of a much bigger firm."

"You said you'll be abroad, dear?" Mrs. B. asked.

"I'll be in the air mostly. I'll still base out of LA, but I'll have responsibility for all the firm's work in the Far East, including Australia and New Zealand. That's a lot of territory."

Well, so much for a trip to the Grand Canyon. "I've always wanted to see Australia," I said.

She reached over to squeeze my hand. "And you will. I'll take you all there." She hesitated. "There's another thing I should mention. There's a lawyer working on the negotiations, and he's the first man I've met in years who I've wanted to spend some real time with. And he feels the same way about me. And even though it's almost ridiculous for people as busy as we are . . . Well, we're actually planning a commitment."

"As in getting married?" Grandpa asked.

Mom made a face. "The word did get mentioned, but we'll probably just find a place together first. Then if —"

"I will have to meet this young man before I can give you permission to start shacking up," Grandpa growled.

"Dad! I am almost forty years old!"

"And still my baby," he said, reaching over to hug her. "About time you found somebody."

I stared at the ceiling so as to avoid eye contact with anybody. As far as I could figure out, everybody at the table with the exception of one particularly virile specimen was already getting laid with considerable regularity.

"Oh, this is wonderful," Mrs. B. chirped. "When will we meet him?"

Mom brushed away a couple of tears. "Soon," she said. "I promise."

Conference rules said that Borsheim couldn't organize practices before mid-February, but nothing said that Jeff couldn't. When we got back from the holidays, he was ready to push hard. And so were the rest of us.

Jeff and I went down to the sports center to talk to Willie-Boy Parker about rates on the batting cage and maybe some advice from the best one-legged batting coach in the hemisphere.

He shook his head. "Too many guys for one night.

You bring down half Tuesday evening and the other half Thursday evening, and I might be able to do you some good."

"Willie-Boy," Jeff said, "we can't afford that much time. Not even if you give us a better rate than last year."

"Stan Olson and I already talked about that. He'll donate one night, I'll donate the other. But you damn well better make good use of it."

We looked at each other. "Uh, that'd be great," I said. "But we can still pay something."

He waved that away. "Forget it. I may be a cripple, and Stan may not be the sharpest pencil in the box, but we've done okay on money. Just be here and be ready to work. Because I might waste my money, but I'm not going to waste my time on anybody who doesn't want to learn."

And so, twice a week, Willie-Boy took apart our stances and our swings, grumping, prodding, and eventually giving his bad-tempered praise as we learned to nail the fastest, nastiest pitches his machines could throw.

National Honor Society had never meant anything to me. I didn't know the requirements, didn't know who selected the candidates, and didn't know who voted them in or out. I was voted in. Sandi wasn't. Sandi went ballistic. I couldn't blame her, because she had a heck of a record: chorus, plays, cheerleading, and a lot of A's.

But that didn't give her the right to march into the principal's office with two other pissed-off girls, where she used *my name* as *the* example of somebody who didn't deserve to be elected.

Nobody bothered to close the door, of course, and with three student aides in the outer office to hear, it wasn't long before the story was all over the halls of how Bull Larsen's sometimes girlfriend, Sandi Watkins, had pretty much announced to the world that she thought he was a brainless jock. Everybody, even those few who disagreed, thought that was funnier than hell.

But I didn't. As a matter of fact, it really pissed me off, and I was barely in control when I caught up with her after the final bell. "Sandi, people are saying you used my name when you talked to Otterholt! Is that goddamn true?"

She spun on me. "And what if it is? Don't I have a right to make a comparison? My grade point's higher than yours, and I've been in a ton of stuff. All you ever did was play stupid baseball!"

"Damn it, Sandi, that's not the —"

"Count the credits in the yearbook, Bull! You just count 'em."

"Hey, I know you should have been elected! But that doesn't give you the right to go into the principal's office and tear me down. I didn't campaign for National Honor Society, and I didn't rig the vote."

"If you really cared about me, you'd refuse to take it. You'd tell them no."

I stared at her, almost too startled to speak. "What difference would that make? That wouldn't change anything."

"Maybe not, but you'd do it. You'd stand up for me."

For a long moment we stood glaring at each other, while God knows how many people looked on. Finally, I said as evenly as I could, "You know, if you'd asked me first, I might have done it. I loved you that goddamn much. But you walked in there and tore me down. So now I'm done with it. Done with you. It hurts like a son of a bitch, but I'm finished. Screw you, Sandi."

"You wish," she shouted after me.

And I turned back a final time. "Not anymore. It'd cost too damned much. You're a whore, Sandi. I just wish I'd figured that out a long time ago."

I didn't go down to the gym to lift weights with the other guys after school. Instead, I sat bundled in my coat in Grandpa's fishing car, watching kids hurrying across the parking lot to cars and buses or pulling collars and scarves around their ears before starting the walk home in the subzero cold. How few of them I knew now — only a handful of the freshmen and sophomores and, outside of Greg Fowler's crowd, not that many juniors. How had that happened? I was popular enough, even looked up to by some of the younger kids. But somehow I'd forgotten to return much of the attention. It'd been simpler just to grin and wave, whenever some kid shouted "Hey, Bull." If they didn't play baseball, they didn't count. And, as far as the girls went, anyone who wasn't Sandi had never really counted. I'd hung with the same crowd, always in love with the same girl, for most of my life. And, God, I was sick of them all.

The heater finally started generating a tendril of heat, and I dropped the fishing car into gear. I drove up to McPherson Park, where I parked near the statue of the general who had been a hero a long time ago. Below me, the land fell away in snow-covered swells that gradually lost definition until they merged with the long roll of cornfields and woodlots disappearing in the gray distance of the western horizon. I remembered Billy running on that day so long ago, running as if his heart would break, over the green swells until the land dropped out from under him. Billy, whom love, friendship, and baseball had all failed to save.

I took a deep breath and tried to think. So what now? Love hadn't done crap for me. My friendships weren't what they'd been, not even with Jeff. That left baseball. Was I kidding myself about that, too?

I studied my hands, grown soft with the winter, the fingernails unchipped, the scrapes and the blisters long healed since the spring a year ago when I'd dropped Phuong's pitch and let Caledonia win the championship. No wonder Jeff no longer talked about how someday we'd play together in the majors. He'd played ball all summer, while I'd let one bad play drive me clear out of town. Even now that we were back at the training, I knew he didn't think that I worked hard enough, that I always quit short of bench-pressing the final weight or stepping into the cage for that one more go at Willie-Boy Parker's batting machine. And he was right. Well, that much I could change.

SPRING –
SENIOR YEAR

Two days after Grandpa's videotape show for Mrs. B., Mrs. Wesley lowered the boom on the Bull. "Neil, it is time for you to show me something of your baseball epic. Hopefully, a big something. Or else, I'm going to have to contact your mother and your grandfather, because you've stalled me just about to the limits of endurance."

I gripped my chest in the general vicinity of the heart. "Not my mother, Mrs. W. She'll fly back here and make an awful, awful scene. I promise."

"Ha! You forget that I was one of your mother's teachers back when we lighted this place with kerosene lamps. I could handle her then, and I can handle her now. You are the problem."

"Yes'm."

"And don't put on that contrite yes'm act for me. I

want writing. Typewritten writing. Pages and pages of it. And I want it by Monday. Then we'll see if we can salvage something approaching comprehensibility out of it, in which case you just might get a passing grade on your senior project."

"It's comprehensive as all get out, Mrs. W. That's part of the problem."

She winced. "Lord, if you were just a little less your mother's kid. *Comprehensible*, Neil. As in intelligent and intelligible. Not *comprehensive*, as in inclusive, capacious, and probably wordy."

"Oh," I said. "Those big words have —"

She stuck a finger in my chest. "Monday. Or it's your throat."

"Yes'm."

I spent the weekend working on my project. Sunday night, I had a mild heart attack when my printer ran out of ink, but Jim had the same model and brought over an extra cartridge. I handed in the first three-quarters of the "epic" to Mrs. W. on Monday morning. "And who says threats aren't a legitimate teaching technique?" she muttered.

"I'm not sure, Mrs. W. Was it —"

"Rhetorical question, Neil." She riffled through the pages. "This *is* rather capacious. Almost depressingly so. I hope every word isn't about baseball."

"I get into a few other things. I'm still working on the part about this season."

"I thought we agreed that we wouldn't worry about this season."

"I know, but I figured since I've gotten this far, I might as well finish."

She shrugged. "Well, all right. That'll be above and beyond for both of us. But if you're willing to work down to the final week, I guess I am, too. Meanwhile . . ." She looked down at my stack of printouts with mild distaste. "We'll try to knock this into shape."

I wanted to leave her cheerful, so I said, "Hey, Mrs. W. Do you remember when you taught us about Tom Swifties?"

"Yes, it was probably the stupidest thing I've done in thirty years of teaching. It took you kids two months to get over it. As I remember, you were one of the worst offenders."

"Well, I made up a new one."

"Please don't make it: 'I broke my leg,' said Tom lamely."

"No, you told us that one. It's: 'I lost my pig,' said Tom disgruntledly."

"Get out of my office," she said. "Now. Before I hurt you."

"Yes'm," I said.

As you might have guessed, I was in a better mood. Not great, but better. Spring training had gone fine, and with a week to go before the first game, we were about as ready as we were going to get. With Billy and Phuong gone, Jeff and I were the only returning regulars, but some of last year's reserves were ready to start and we had a real good bunch of juniors up from the jayvees. Finally, we had the best two sophomores since I (and Phuong and Jeff) had made varsity: Wes Halloway's little brother, Bill, and Todd Ronchetti, the latest of the clan who'd played ball for Shipley since Babe Ruth was a pup. The lineup looked like this:

1.	No. 22	Todd Ronchetti, so., center field
2.	No. 19	Terry Walters, sr., second base
3.	No. 17	Jeff Hanson, sr., shortstop
4.	No. 10	Neil Larsen, sr., catcher
5.	No. 14	Greg Fowler, jr., first base
6.	No. 21	Bill Halloway, so., right field
7.	No. 35	Fred Schoonover, jr., left field
8.	No. 31	Jack Reisman, sr., third base
9.	pitcher	

Our hitting and defense looked solid, and our pitching was better than I expected. Ed Parkenham had settled into his role as our ace, putting aside his feigned accent and all the goofy stuff about estates in England. Behind him, at least for the moment, we had Ben McConnell, a senior transfer student, who'd shown up on the first day of practice to surprise us with a very respectable fastball. He had only a mediocre curve and a change that I wouldn't throw a dog, but both were showing promise.

With Phil Stroetz, we had the best closer since Marc Tobin, but there wasn't a whole lot of other talent in the pen with the exception of Ms. Sally Eckes, a pug-nosed, frizzy-headed sophomore who looked about twelve. Normally, Shipley girls play softball, even when it means finishing somewhere between ten and fifteen games behind the Herons. But Sally's knuckleball didn't knuckle when she threw it underhand. So, she tried out for baseball and made the team, because nobody had ever seen a high school knuckleballer of either sex who could get one over the plate twice in a row. Sally could — sometimes even three times in a row. Still, catching her dancing, dipping knuckleball was the hardest thing I'd ever done behind the plate. It worried me enough to bring it up with Borsheim and Jeff when we had our weekly meeting.

"Can she get batters out or not?" Borsheim asked.

"She can get them to swing, Coach. Problem is what happens when she comes in with runners on. I'm not sure I want to risk the passed balls then."

"Well, you're supposed to be the best catcher in the conference. I guess you're going to have to prove it again."

"Second best," I said. "Polster was all-conference."

"Only because he caught for the conference champions. I know better and you know better. So how do you suggest we use Sally?"

"I want to start her."

"Start her? She doesn't have the strength to go five or

243

six innings. She probably isn't strong enough to go more than three."

"Two or three will be all we want, because even a knuckleball's vulnerable second time through the order. And she's got nothing to back it up, Coach. No fastball, no curve. But if she can give us two or three scoreless, we can go to the pen."

He leaned back, studying me. "Cap, what do you think?"

Jeff shrugged. "If Bull thinks he can make it work, I've got no problem. Her fielding's pretty good. Better than Park's."

"Well, you use that to get Parkenham's attention. Okay, Bull, they're your pitchers. But remember, she's only a sophomore."

"And a girl," I said.

"Don't," he said, "ever say that again. Cripes, we'll get sued."

"Yeah," Jeff said. "And that babe you know on the Herons will probably break both your legs."

I laughed. Yeah, Bev would do something emphatic. I ought to write her sometime.

Jeff wanted me to make the speech, but he was team captain and that made it his job. He put it off until Borsheim told him it had to be done before our Saturday opener against Walthrop. So that Friday after practice, he called everybody together.

I handed him Billy's uniform shirt, and he draped it

over his arm. "Coach, Bull, and me thought it'd be right if we retired Billy's number. And I, uh, got elected to say something about Billy. That's kind of tough because I keep expecting to see him at the back, wearing that smart-ass smirk he always had when people were trying to be serious." He paused to clear his throat. "But when it came to the real game, Billy always went all out. And that was kind of how he lived, too. No brakes. Everything to the limit . . . Like some of the rest of us, I think he played ball to keep himself sane." He gestured toward the field. "Because things made sense here. And a lot of times they didn't in other places. At least not in Billy's life."

He looked down at the shirt. "Funny thing. Billy always wanted to be thirteen, but we never had the right shirt for him. So, it was always, 'Wait until next season, Billy.' Now there isn't going to be any next season for Billy. . . . But I'll tell you, if he were here to wear this number or any other number, he'd do his best to win the championship. And I guess that's what we ought to do." He looked at me. "Bull, you want to say anything?"

I opened my mouth, ready to say something about how I was sorry that Billy and I had been on the outs toward the end, but the words caught in my throat. Which surprised me, because I figured I'd dealt with most of that already. So I just shook my head and looked down, blinking back the tears.

I was surprised to hear Jim speak up, his voice strong when Jeff and I had choked. "You know," he said,

"Billy'd be embarrassed by all this. He'd say, 'Hey, stop with all the talk. Let's just go and beat the crap out of the other guys and then we'll all feel better.' And even if I just warm up pitchers, I think I agree." There was a smattering of applause.

Jeff took a deep breath. "Jim's right. Tomorrow let's beat the crap out of Walthrop. For Billy and because it'll make us feel better."

We put the hurt on Walthrop, 11–5, then three days later, on Mosinee, 9–6. It was the beginning of a pattern. Without Phuong and the Mule, we were bound to give up more runs, but we had some serious offense to make up for it. Including, I might mention, yours truly, the league's leader in home runs and RBI's from game one through most of the season.

We were 7–2 and Caledonia was 8–1 when we went up to play them the first time. They had the banners up, the fans out in force, and Rob McHugh's little brother, Jamie, on the mound. He still looked like a grade-school kid, but if he had a weakness, we couldn't find it. We didn't hit for shit, while they took apart Ed Parkenham, Ben McConnell, Phil Stroetz, and just about everybody else in our bull pen. Final score 13–2, with their second string finishing up.

Jeff's knuckles were swollen from punching lockers. "Bush!" he yelled. "What the hell do we have to do to keep from being bush? Everybody here got so damned intimidated that we let them take it to us and take it to us until they were so damned bored they lost interest! Did you see what that jerk Polster was doing in the last inning? He was sitting on the bench reading *Mad Magazine!*"

Nobody said anything. At last, Jeff turned away. "Bush," he muttered. "Goddamn bush."

He tried to resign as captain the next day. "Let Bull do it. We're already pretty much cocaptains, anyway. Let him do it all."

Borsheim leaned back. "Do you want to play ball?"

"Hell, yes, I want to play ball. I just don't want to be responsible for how anybody else plays ball. I'm sick of it."

"So, you're just going to perform for the scouts and to hell with the team."

"I'll bust my ass for this team, Coach. But face it, this team is never going to win the big ones. We don't have the talent, and we don't have the guts. We —"

Borsheim held up a palm. "No, we do have the talent. Maybe not as much as Caledonia, but we've got enough. The guts . . . Well, you guys are going to have to answer that yourselves. But if you seniors start quitting on me mentally, I'll start building for next year. I'll play the juniors because they are a good bunch, and they're still willing to believe." He looked at me. "You got anything to say?"

I hesitated, glancing at Jeff, who'd turned his back to us and was leaning dejectedly against a file cabinet.

"Not a whole lot, I guess. Except that I still think we need Jeff as captain and, no matter what anybody else thinks, I still think we can beat Caledonia."

Jeff turned. "Oh, come on, Bull! They've got a two-game lead on us, and they're going to keep winning. You can bet on it. When is everybody going to wake up to the fact that when we lost Phuong we lost any chance of winning the championship? Those kids you've got — Ed, Ben, Phil, Sally — they can pitch their hearts out, but they're still not going to add up to one Phuong. And meanwhile, Caledonia has Hank Lutz and Jamie McHugh."

I shrugged. "I'm not saying we can catch them. Maybe we can't. But we can beat them the last game of the year. And whether they're champions or not by that time, we're still going to have some bragging rights."

He stared at me stubbornly. Borsheim cleared his throat. "Go take a long walk. Both of you. Tomorrow, you can tell me how you want to play it."

We parked the fishing car near the statue of General McPherson and walked down over the green swells descending toward the edge of town and the farmland beyond. A warm wind blew from the west, carrying the smell of drying fields, new grass, and the coming of summer. "Remember how Billy loved it up here?" I asked.

"Yeah, poor Billy. I really wanted to win that championship for him."

"It works that way in the movies, Jeff. I don't think in real life."

"Yeah, maybe not. But if Phuong had stuck with us, we could have done it."

"You know, you're going to have to forgive him one of these days. Phuong was good for the team. He gave as much as anybody. Except you, of course."

"And you."

"Well, I don't know. I quit on you last summer. If I had stuck around, maybe we could have trained some pitchers."

He didn't reply, and I knew he'd thought of that, too. We sat on a picnic table, not saying anything. Jeff shook his head, as if to clear it. "Oh, hell. I know baseball doesn't mean anything. Not compared to helping sick people in Vietnam. It's just that we were so damned —"

"Stop driving yourself nuts. What do we do now?"

He sighed. "Well, I guess we play a little ball. Do the best we can even if we can't catch them. As you said, if we beat them that last game, we'll at least have some bragging rights."

"I always thought you were an optimist. Hell, they're not ten-feet tall. With a little luck, we can still catch them."

"Well, they're about nine-and-a-half feet tall. But I suppose you're right."

"Damn right I am. Besides, I've got a scholarship to win and I might as well get a championship while I'm at it."

He nodded. "Yeah, and you are better than Jake Polster. . . . God, he pisses me off. Joe, Hank, Gary, the other guys, they're okay. But Polster is a jerk. When Stroetz saw him reading that *Mad Magazine*, I thought he was going to grab a bat and go after him."

"Have to hit him a dozen times to find a vital spot. The only way we're going to get his attention is by whipping them."

"That'd be a reason to do it."

"So are you going to stay on as captain?"

He shrugged. "I guess. We've gone this far, might as well take it the rest of the way. . . . That's if anybody wants me besides you and Borsheim."

"They do," I said.

The team was gathered by the outside doors when Jeff and I pulled into the south parking lot the next morning. "Is this a lynch mob or what?" Jeff said.

"I don't know."

They shifted around uncomfortably while we crossed the parking lot. Greg had been elected spokesman, and he stepped a little out in front of the rest. "Uh, Jeff, we kinda heard that you were thinking about quitting as captain. And, well, we were going to tell you that we wouldn't blame you if you did. Because we played horseshit in Caledonia. But if you stick with us, we'll pick it up. Practice harder. Play better."

Jeff bit his lip. "Yeah. Well, I've already thought about it, and I guess I'm not a quitter. We had a lousy game.

Let's just worry about the next one. I'll see you at practice."

He started moving through the crowd, but then he stopped. "Okay, damn it! I'm pissed at you guys and even more pissed at myself. Because maybe I let you think you were better than you are. But I will not settle for any more bush-league ball. And neither will you. You still want me as captain, you gotta know that I'm gonna be all over anybody who dogs it, screws up, or wimps out on this team!" He glared at them.

They looked at each other. Sally wrinkled her nose in a frown. "Well, we all know that. That's why you're captain, isn't it?" There were a lot of nods.

"I don't know about you guys," I said, "but I've got to get to class. Let's just forget the speech-making and play some ball this afternoon. I think everybody's better at that, anyway."

And the next day we thumped, and I mean *thumped*, Lein's Forks, the third best team in the conference. Jeff had four hits and I had three, including my ninth home run of the year. Final score, 12–1.

Jeff never made another speech, and he didn't have to, because we won and kept winning. So did Caledonia, until Mosinee finally tripped them up, cutting their lead to a game.

With two games to go in the season, Jeff was scheduled for another look by a college scout. And I was pissed. So far this spring, he'd stayed after practice six times to show off his stuff for scouts. I hadn't been asked once, although — nice guy that I was — I always stuck around to do the catching. Sally, who had a first-class crush on Jeff, usually stayed to play first, and a few of the kids who always hung around practice, hoping for a nod or a chore from one of the players, jumped at the chance to shag flies. Someday, maybe they could say they'd chased a ball for the great Jeff Hanson. Me, I wanted more.

The day's scout, this one from USC, watched while Borsheim hit about a hundred grounders to Jeff at short. He fielded every ball within human reach, burning them over to Sally, who tossed them back to me. And, *whack*, Borsheim would hit another.

When the scout was satisfied, Jeff came in to bat, and Sally danced over to the mound. She didn't have anything special except the knuckler, but she could get a fastball of sorts over the plate. The scout watched Jeff lace liners to left, right, and center, and then called, "Okay, I've got it, Miss." Sally made a face at him before tossing him the ball, but he didn't seem to notice.

The scout took off his jacket, spent a moment testing the mound, and then threw Jeff a nasty curve. Jeff popped it up. The scout picked up another ball from the dozen by the mound and threw the curve again. Jeff got it but not much of it. He tightened his stance, and succeeded in hitting the next one more or less solidly.

In all, the scout threw him maybe two dozen curves. Jeff hit about half of them, but none really on the screws.

"Okay," the scout said, "we'll need a little work on the curve. Coach, could you come in and throw him some hard stuff?"

Jeff swore under his breath. "Did you see how that curve broke down and in? Weird."

"Relax, you're doing fine," I said. Turkey.

Borsheim threw about twenty respectable heaters, and Jeff hit nearly every one. Finally, the scout said thanks to everyone, shook Jeff's hand, and took Borsheim aside to quiz him. "Go ahead," Jeff said. "No guts, no glory."

But I hesitated. Borsheim waved me over. "Mr. Clark, we've got a pretty good catcher here, too. Neil Larsen."

The scout looked up. "Oh, sure." He stuck out a hand. "I saw you hit a homer the other day. Maybe we'll have a look at you next time." He turned back to Borsheim. "That pitcher you had last year. The one with the funny name. Now what exactly is the story on him?"

Next time. Sure.

Borsheim called me into his office as I was leaving the locker room. "Bull, these guys see an awful lot of players. They just can't try out everybody."

I stared at the floor until I was sure I could control my voice. "Coach, just what do I have to do? I'm hitting three-forty, and I've got thirteen homers and thirty-two ribbies in eighteen games. Hardly anybody tries to steal on me anymore. I've only had three passed balls all year, and that's with a knuckleballer on the staff. Just what the hell do I have to do to get them to pay some attention to me?"

He sighed. "Bull, you're good. You're very good. And people do know about you. Stevens Point, River Falls, and Superior. They've all called, and they'll probably all offer you some kind of tuition help. And I think a few people still remember me at Stout. I'll be happy to talk to them."

"They're the little league, Coach. I'm sorry, but you know that, too. How do I get into Arizona State or USC or New Mexico? Hell, I'm a better student than Jeff. I'm even in the National Honor Society."

"I know," he said. "I nominated you. Look, son, all we can do is keep hoping. Maybe one of the big schools will come around. Personally, I think you'd be a plus in any program. Just keep hitting the ball. Come the end of the season, we'll send around your stats and that tape we shot."

I nodded and turned for the door. "Bull," he said. "Walthrop, tomorrow. They're nothing special, but we've got to be careful with them. You want to go with Ben or Sally for the start?"

I took a ragged breath, trying to focus on the question. "Sally," I said. "If she can do three, we'll have everybody else that much fresher for Friday. Who's Caledonia play tomorrow?"

He sighed. "McArthur, and all the talent up there

seems to be over on the girls' team. If Caledonia wins, they clinch it."

"Unless we beat them by twelve runs or so on Friday to get the tie-breaker back on our side."

He smiled ruefully. "Well, some things aren't possible. Not against Lutz and McHugh. But even if we don't win that championship, we've had a good season."

Sally was perfect for three against Walthrop. Perfect, that is, if you didn't count the three walks she gave up when even she couldn't get the knuckler to cooperate. We were up 4–0, and I told Borsheim that we could stick with her for another inning. Bad choice, since the first two Walthrop hitters in the fourth nailed her with a double and a run-scoring single.

I signaled Borsheim and jogged out to the mound. "Why'd you do that?" she snapped. "Those were the first two hits I gave up."

"Yeah, and you're about to give up a bunch more. You're tired and the knuckler's straightening out on you."

She glared at me, all scrap and fire. "My dad says it works better when I'm tired."

I grinned at her. "You know, I am really going to miss you. You are a kick in the ass."

She was complimented but wouldn't let it show. "Kick your ass, anyway."

Borsheim reached the mound. "Ben?" he said to me.

"No, they've only got one aboard. Let's bring in Pat and then Fitz. They're both seniors and this'll probably be their last chance. And that'll keep Ben and Phil fresh for Friday."

"Okay, but we don't want this one getting away on us."

"I think we'll be okay. I feel a homer coming on."

"Careful, son. The gods strike people dead for less." He signaled the pen.

"Hey, I want to pitch Friday, too," Sally said. "Nobody's talking about me."

"You're always on the list," Borsheim said. "Take a hike, now."

As she started toward the bench, Jeff yelled, "Good job, Sally." She gave a flounce of her hair and followed it with a pirouette. The crowd was appreciative as always.

Pat and Fitz did what I told them to do: get the ball over and let the defense play defense. Walthrop managed two more runs, but we rang up six more, including three on my fourteenth homer of the year. Final score: 10–3.

By this time, I guess everybody had just assumed that Caledonia would stuff McArthur to lock up the championship. So when Borsheim came out of his office with a big grin on his face, nobody reacted for a second. "Guys, McArthur did it. Three–two on a home run by a kid named Herkert. We are tied and playing for the championship!"

The place went nuts. Jeff shouted to me. "Herkert? Isn't that the name of that babe you know? Did she play in reverse drag or something?"

I was searching for a name. "No, that'd be her little brother Donny, I think."

"Well, you are going to have to write him and the whole family one hell of a thank-you note for us."

"Yeah, I should." Really.

I got flowers from Mom, which was definitely a first, with a card reading: "Good Luck on Friday! See you at graduation."

What the heck was I supposed to do with flowers? I gave them to Mrs. B. when Grandpa and I went over to eat an early supper on Senior Projects night. "Oh, Neil, they're beautiful. I'll put them on the sideboard so we can enjoy them right along with supper. Thank you so much." She kissed me.

"Uh, sure," I said, thinking that maybe I should have given them to Mrs. Wesley, who wouldn't have kissed me and definitely deserved the thanks after all the editing she'd done. I'd been up until midnight five nights running, doing the rewriting, and now had the "epic" in a binder and ready to go on display. Only the last page or two had yet to be written, and those only because I didn't know the end of the story just yet.

We ate, and when a horn beeped outside, I excused myself. "That's Jeff," I said. "We'll see you at school."

* * *

All the seniors at Shipley High have to do senior projects. The genius set lays out some pretty incredible science stuff in the gym: robots, rockets, lasers, and pages of formulas that no one with an IQ below 180 can understand. The artsy crowd shows off their sculpture, painting, and jewelry in the cafeteria. But the best show is down in the tech-ed wing, where the shop kids are showing off their stock cars, four-wheelers, wood splitters, and just about everything else you can weld or bolt together. Meanwhile, time is edging by in the library, where the written projects and their authors are mildewing nicely, thank you.

I leaned against my table and yawned. Jeff drifted over, ignoring the rule about staying close to our projects. "Do we really have to stay here until eight?" he asked.

"Eight-thirty."

"Eight-thirty! Everything in food science will be eaten by then."

"Yep."

He idly turned a few pages of my epic. "A lot in here about me?"

"Nothing but the truth."

"That's grim."

"Don't worry, it didn't take a lot of space to polish you off. By the way, Mr. A. is making threatening gestures at you."

"Yeah, that figures. I'll see you later."

He sauntered back to stand by his timeline showing

the history of the Olympic games. He'd wanted to do baseball, of course, but Mr. Aschbrock had insisted on something more "historically significant." Well, not everybody could understand.

Crossing the edge of the parking lot, my spikes crunching on the gravel, I gazed up, gauging the depth of the sky. Perfect, deep blue, and cloudless so a pop-up would stand out no matter how high it rose. Out in the bull pen, Jim was arranging equipment and checking the first-aid kit. I waved, and he grinned and gave me a thumbs-up. Then, at the edge of the field I'd played on a hundred times and more, I paused. I was completely and absolutely right where I'd always wanted to be: playing for a championship against the biggest, baddest dogs in the conference.

I knew if I turned around to look at the stands, I'd find Grandpa, Mrs. B., Willie-Boy, and maybe a hundred other people I knew. But I didn't look, because that wasn't the way you did it. You came to play ball, and for the next seven innings, only the people on the field mattered.

I inspected the area around home plate and then sauntered out to join Stan Olson at the mound. "Hey, Stan."

"How ya doing, Bull? Gonna whup 'em today?"

And after three years, I changed the formula. "Yeah, we are, Stan. All the way to hell and gone."

He stared at me for a long moment. Then he grinned.

"Okay. The field's good as it can get. So I've done my part." He stuck out a hand. "Good luck."

"Thanks, Stan. Thanks for everything. If you see Willie-Boy, tell him thanks, too."

"Gonna sit right by him. See if our money did any good."

Borsheim came striding across the parking lot, clipboard in hand and scowl in place, while the varsity hustled by him. Jeff and I joined him at the bench. "Okay," he said, consulting the clipboard. "Who do we see first?"

Doug Rasmussen struck out leading off for Caledonia, but then Gary Melcher beat out a slow roller to Jack Reisman at third. Not a good start. I crouched, watching Gary, as Jake Polster stepped in. Sure enough, Gary took off for second on the first pitch, and he could still do what almost nobody else tried anymore. It was close, though, and I thought for a second that my throw actually got there ahead of him. The umpire didn't. Gary called time to brush himself off. Jeff looked at me and held thumb and forefinger a millimeter apart.

We got Jake on a couple more fastballs and a deadfish change, which seriously pissed him off. Then we went to work on Joe Spence. And although Ed Parkenham had grown a lot as a pitcher, he still wasn't up to getting out Caledonia's biggest dog. Ed threw a perfect curve at Joe's knees, and Joe went down and muscled it out for his fourteenth homer of the year. 2–0.

With two outs in the bottom of the first and Jeff aboard on a single, I came up intent on evening the score and going one up in home runs. But Hank Lutz threw me a sequence of curves that had me swinging out of my shoes. Good pitches, good psychology, and a big K for Big Hank.

Nothing much happened in the second, but in the top of the third Jake parked one of Ed's fastballs to get back at us for the dead fish. 3–0. We didn't do crap in our half of the inning.

In the top of the fourth, it looked like they were about to lay the big one on Ed and the rest of us when they loaded the bases with one out on a single, an error, and a walk. I went out to talk to him. "How you doing, Ed?"

"For shit. I don't know what to do with these guys."

"Just throw what I tell you to."

"Yeah, but I just walked a guy on four straight."

"Two of 'em were strikes," I lied. "I'll tell you what I told Phuong a long time ago: I'm going to put up my mitt and you're going to hit it. That's all we're going to do. Play catch."

"And you think that's going to work?"

I grinned at him. "Guaranteed."

I jogged back to the plate, took my place, and put the grin on again for Doug Rasmussen. "Curve down and away, Dougie."

I set up where I'd said it'd be, and watched him swing for a high inside fastball. "Shit," he said. "That's not the way it's done. It's high and in and then down and away."

261

"I always forget that," I said. I fed him a dead fish for a second swinging strike, and then went back low and away with another curve. He chopped that one to Terry Walters at second, who picked it clean and flipped it to Jeff coming across the bag. Jeff leaped high out of the way of the sliding runner, firing the ball in the same motion to Greg at first to get Doug and the double play by a step.

Terry led off our half of the fourth with a grounder that did a seeing-eye number through the right side. Jeff followed with a nasty chopper that really should have gotten through. But Gary Melcher, who probably had the best glove of any second baseman in the league, flagged it down and forced Terry at second. My turn.

I'd been watching Hank's pitch sequence. Both Terry and Jeff had hit curves low and away, following the usual high and tight fastball. Good pitches, and by rights the bases should have been empty. So, why should he change except that he'd fed me nothing but curveballs the first time?

Jake Polster gave me a narrow glance as I stepped in. Right now, everybody was guessing. And my guess was that Jake would call a fastball down the pipe before going to nibbling with the curve.

When you guess right, there's not a worse feeling in the world than when you miss it anyway. But I didn't. Not a gram of it, and everyone in the park knew it. I gave myself a hitch step to watch it go before I ran. It

262

cleared the left-field fence long before I got to first, and I dropped into my home-run trot. When I crossed the plate, Polster growled, "Lucky guess, Larsen."

"Nah, I can read you like a book, Jake. Big print, nothing longer than four letters. Lots of dirty pictures."

He didn't get that for a second, then he snarled, "Hey, screw you, jerk."

We were still down 3–2, but Greg Fowler and Bill Halloway followed with singles to put runners on first and third. Caledonia's coach went out to the mound, and I was sure we were going to see Jamie McHugh. But he only said a few words to Hank and then jogged back to the bench. Hank spent a long minute grooming his landing point and then messing with the rosin bag. Then he looked up and grinned. "Heat," I said to Jeff. "Tell Fred to watch for heat."

But we couldn't get his attention and — *bam, bam* — he was down two strikes, then gone on a curve. With Jack Reisman, Hank didn't even bother to throw the curve. Heat, three straight, and we were back on defense still down by a run.

Leading off the top of the fifth, Gary Melcher beat out another infield hit, making him the luckiest guy on the field. And, of course, we both knew he'd try to steal yet another one on the Bull. Question was, when? I had Ed throw over to keep him close, and then signaled for a fastball low inside. Jake Polster took it for a strike. "How about that change again, Larsen? I've got something I'd like to do with it."

"In your dreams, Jake." I watched Gary wiggle another six inches out on his lead. Second pitch? Or was he just testing Ed's move? I signaled fastball outside and clenched my fist. Ed fired the ball with everything he had, and I had it and was rearing up. Jake saw Gary leaning the wrong way for the fatal split second and tried to block me, but I threw my left elbow into his ribs and let go the peg to first. Gary was diving back, his hand outstretched, but the throw was there, and Greg's tag brushed between Gary's fingers and the bag. "Out!" the umpire yelled.

Polster and I glared at each other. "You two, just cool off," the home plate umpire growled. "One and one. Play ball."

Jake chopped the next one to Jeff at short, and we had only Joe Spence to get by to get to our half of the fifth. But Joe measured the third pitch, and hit it a long, long way. 4–2.

While Joe circled the bases, I signaled for Borsheim and trudged out to the mound. Jeff joined us. Ed looked on the point of tears, and I felt sorry for him. But I knew my job. "He's done, Coach. He pitched a good game, but they've seen all his stuff. Let's try to get out of this inning with Ben and then go to Phil for the last two."

"You got it," Borsheim said. He took the ball from Ed and slapped him on the butt. "Good job. We'll get 'em yet."

Ben came on, gave up a single and then walked the

next batter when he tried to nip a corner on a 3–2 pitch. God, how exciting did we have to make this game? I took a step out in front of the plate and pointed to the center of my mitt. "Where I call it, Ben." He nodded sheepishly. That worked better, and we got out of it without any more damage.

Hank got Ben on a ground ball leading off our half of the inning, but Todd Ronchetti and Terry Walters hit him for consecutive hard singles to put runners at first and third. That was it for Hank, who'd probably pitched more innings than anybody else in the conference over the last couple of months. Jamie McHugh came in for his big shot at glory, and Jeff hit his first fastball to left to score Todd and move Terry to third. 4–3. The throw from left missed the cutoff man, and Jeff scooted into second. Second and third, one out, my turn again.

But they didn't really let me have a turn, pitching me low and away to walk me on five pitches. I jogged down to first, spent a moment kicking dirt out of my spikes, and then gazed over at Gary Melcher at second and Denny Panzer at short. You might get one out, guys, but watch your nuts because I'm coming hard and high. I took an extra half step on my lead and waited for the first pitch to Greg. And Greg did just what I'd been afraid of: he hit a roller to short. I was pounding toward second, my vision jumpy with the effort. Denny fielded the ball and flipped it to Gary coming across the bag. I went as far out of the base path as I dared, but Gary was much too quick, his throw singing over my head before I was fully extended in the slide. They had Greg by plenty. Damn.

Phil Stroetz came on in the top of the sixth, gave up a bloop single, and then buckled down to get two strike-outs and an easy fly to left. When he came off the mound, he pointed at Jake Polster. "Next inning, friend."

"Cool it, Phil," I said. "No time to get tossed now. Let's worry about getting the run."

Even with two at bats to go and only down by a run, I was getting that sinking sensation every ballplayer knows — the feeling you get when you realize that as much as you try to pump up, it's not going to work. They are going to beat you, because they are better.

I looked over at Jeff, who was talking fast to Fred Schoonover and Jack Reisman. They nodded and picked up their bats. "What'd you tell them?"

"I'm not dead sure, but I think McHugh tips his curve by readjusting his cap. He never does it before throwing a cutter or straight heat."

"I never noticed that."

"Well, as I said, I'm not dead sure. I just wish I'd had time to tell Bill."

Bill Halloway hit a soft liner to Denny Panzer at short for the first out, and Fred took his place in the box. "Wait for it," Jeff muttered. "Wait for it. There. See how he touched the bill of his cap?"

And sure enough, the McHugh kid threw a curve. And it was a good one, but Fred nailed it down the left-field line, where it bounced around obligingly in the corner, giving him time to leg it all the way to third ahead of Joe Spence's throw.

Jack went up watching for the same tip-off, got it, and drove the curve to center, deep enough to score Fred. 4–4. We were off the bench to mob him when he came in. Maybe we could do it. Maybe we even would.

Polster went out to snarl at McHugh. "Oh, oh," Jeff said. "I think Jake knows the tip. Probably's been trying to cure him of it."

"Yeah, could be," I said. "Okay, go get 'em, Phil. Two-out boomer."

But Phil Stroetz was full of adrenaline and a bit too fast on a no-tip-off curve, popping it straight up. Jake waved everybody away and took it himself. He grinned at Phil. "See *you* next inning, *friend*."

I caught Phil's warm-ups and then went out for a quick word before Jake stepped in. "Look, just forget all the crap with Polster. Let's just —"

"I don't want to forget. He's a jerk."

"That's no news. But just forget about that for now and throw what I tell you to."

"I want to throw heat."

"Okay, but where I tell you to."

I went back to the plate, thinking he'd gotten the word. But he hadn't, and when I called for one low and outside, he threw it straight down the pipe. Jake, who might have been a jerk but was a damned good hitter, hammered it into the gap in left center and hoofed into second with a standing double. Joe Spence knocked the weighted ring off his bat and started for the plate. I called time, signaled to Borsheim, and headed for the mound.

Phil was fuming, which wasn't going to do anybody a damned bit of good. Everything he threw would be lunch meat for the biggest, baddest dog of all. Short of hitting Joe or walking him, I saw only one thing we could do. "I want to bring in Sally," I said.

Jeff, Phil, and Borsheim stared. "Now wait just a god-damn second — " Phil snapped.

"Joe's never seen her, Coach," I said. "Maybe he's never even seen a knuckleball. But I'll tell you one thing for sure, he's never seen one as good as hers."

Borsheim looked at Jeff. "Cap?"

And Jeff grinned, because what we were about to do was just crazy enough to work. "Sure," he said. "Why not?"

Phil started to supply some answers on the "why not," but Borsheim had already signaled the pen. And Sally, who'd been throwing dispiritedly to Jim, stared at us, and then ran all the way in. The noise of the crowd rose, confused, and then people started cheering. What the hell, lay it all out, Shipley.

Borsheim and Jeff left me alone with her. "You know

how to throw it, I don't," I said. "So do it just like your daddy taught you, and I'll try to catch it."

She bit her lip and nodded, looking very small, very young, and *very* determined. I grinned at her. "Relax. It's only a game."

"Yeah, *right*," she said. "Go make like you're calling a pitch, huh?"

I laughed, pulled her cap an inch down over her red curls, and jogged back to the plate.

Joe stepped into the box. "What the hey, Bull?"

"Oh, you'll like her stuff, Joe. It's sweet."

"Okay, bring it on."

The knuckler came in, and I heard Joe grunt as he swung over it. He stepped out. "Knuckleball?"

"Yep."

"Jeez, I heard you had a girl on the team, but I didn't know what she threw. Huh." He stepped in, and I prayed Sally could get two in a row across. She did, and Joe missed again. He fixed her with a long gaze.

"Hang in there, Joe. You'll get it," I said.

He grunted, and when the next one came in, he hit it a ton. Foul. "Shit," he muttered. "That would've been the game."

Not quite, I thought, but probably. I gritted my teeth and called the knuckleball again. And Joe missed. He swore, and then did what made him, at least, worthy of being a champion. He touched the bill of his cap to her.

I wiped the sweat from my face and settled my mask

again. Out on the mound, Sally was trying her damnedest to look nonchalant after striking out the league's best hitter. Beyond her, Jake Polster glared at me, hands on hips. Screw him.

Dewey Carlson, their right fielder and a pretty good bat, stepped in. "You ever try to catch one of these knuckleballs, Dewey? Hell, I never know where they're going. And funny thing, they really hurt, too. Must be the funny spin on them."

"Can it, Bull."

"Sure." I called the knuckleball.

He missed and missed the next one, even though it was a foot outside. But as I said, he was a pretty good hitter, and when Sally's next knuckler didn't knuckle, he looped it over Jeff's head into short left. And though Polster was no speedster, he figured he was fast enough and came around third, steaming for the plate. Fred Schoonover hit Jeff at the cutoff, and Jeff spun and fired the ball home. And a lot of me wanted to put Jake Polster on his ass, but instead I matadored him. *Olé*, Jake. "You're out!" the ump shouted.

"Third!" Sally shrieked. I looked up to see Dewey trying to hustle into third, and I threw a ball I probably shouldn't have thrown, because there was too much risk of sailing it into left. But I was right on the money, and Jack Reisman slapped the tag down to nail him. Double play and still tied 4–4 with us coming to bat in the last half inning of regulation.

We'd never seen Mike Schultz, their closer, because

they'd never bothered to bring him in against us. But we knew him by reputation. Fast, mean, and some more mean. Still, we had the top of the order up and couldn't ask for a better shot. And maybe it'd be our only real shot; they were a lot deeper in the pen and on the bench than we were, and everything would be in their favor if we went into extra innings.

But Todd was gone on three swinging strikes, and Terry hit a comebacker to the mound that Schultz tossed casually to first. Jeff's turn. Polster jogged out to have a quick word with Schultz, and then signaled the first and third basemen to move over to guard the lines. I took a final swing with the weighted bat and knelt in the on-deck circle as Jeff took strike one on the outside corner. He was watching the first baseman and the right fielder but being cool about it. He took ball one and then ball two as they tried to sucker him. And from seeing him play a thousand times, I knew exactly what he was thinking. The next pitch came inside, almost certainly ball three, but Jeff hit it inside out, slashing it over the leaping first baseman's head and down the right-field line. Dewey had a long run, and Jeff legged it into an easy double. Gary Melcher took the throw at second, glanced at Jeff, and then tossed it to Schultz.

The ump wanted to inspect the ball for grass stains, so I took another couple of practice cuts before heading for the plate. Jeff gazed in at me as I stepped into the box, and I could feel the power of his will — our will — surge like a high-voltage pulse between us.

271

The Caledonia coach jogged to the mound to talk to Schultz. Polster and a couple of the infielders joined him. After a minute, the ump started out, but they broke it up. Jake had a final word with Schultz and then jogged back to the plate. Oh, shit, I thought, they wouldn't, would they? I stepped in again, already feeling the disappointment welling in my gut. Jake remained standing, holding his mitt a yard outside. I leveled my bat, cocked it, and waited. Schultz glanced back at Jeff, who'd taken a cautious lead at second, and then lobbed the first intentional ball. "You're chickenshit, Polster," I said.

"Take it as a compliment. It's all you're going to get out of this game. We're gonna kick some ass next inning." He tossed the ball back.

I stepped out and looked over at Borsheim. He shrugged and turned to say something to Danny Jensen, the fast little sophomore who'd come in to run for me. I stepped back in, watched the second ball sail in like a big, fat balloon, and then stepped out again while Jake threw it back. I took a couple of practice cuts, not knowing exactly why, and then glanced at Jeff. And I knew. Maybe he told me through that high-voltage connection between us. Or maybe it was just all the countless hours of practice, all the sore muscles, all the games we'd won and lost, all the disappointment of falling just a little short all those years. Screw these guys, I thought. I am not coming out of this game for some pinch runner. I'm going to win it or lose it right here and now.

I stepped back in, not letting a twitch of emotion show on my face. Jeff was off, digging hard for third, as Schultz came to the plate. I took a half step to my right and swung — not hard because I had to reach as far as my arms and my bat allowed — but hard enough. The ball cracked on the bat and sailed two feet over Gary Melcher's desperate leap to bloop into center. And I was pounding up the line, my head down, feeling Gary already lunging after the ball, his concentration on spinning and firing it to first, because he was smart and knew he'd never get Jeff, not now, but that he might just get me. Ahead first base glimmered, impossibly distant. I dove for it, feeling myself suspended in air for an immeasurably long second as the first baseman stretched for Gary's throw. And then I hit, my hand slamming on the bag a microsecond before the ball smacked into his glove. The ump yelled, "Safe!" and Shipley's stands went nuts.

For a long moment, I lay there, my eyes closed, tasting the grit of the dirt on my lips and letting myself have that moment alone to know what it felt like to be a champion at last. When I got up, Jeff was wrestling his way free of the whooping crowd around home plate and running toward me. "Bull!" he yelled. "Damn it, Bull, we did it!" He threw his arms around me.

I was laughing. "Yeah, we did, didn't we?"

"Wow," he yelled, "does this feel good or what?"

"Yeah, it does," I said. "Get used to it, you'll have a lot more."

"And you will, too, Bull. You and me, buddy. We're

gonna set the world on fire, and we ain't never gonna die."

The crowd of fans swallowed us, pulled us apart. I took the congratulations and handshakes and smiled a lot as I pushed through to the Caledonia bench.

Joe Spence greeted me. "Hey, hell of a game, Bull." He glanced back to see where his coach was. "They should have let you swing for the fence. That intentional walk stuff is chickenshit."

"Part of the game, I guess."

"Yeah, maybe. But it's still chickenshit. Well, we tied on the homers again. No next time, I guess."

"Guess not. Where you going in the fall?"

"Going to play some football for Purdue. The team sucks, but the scholarship's good."

"No baseball?"

"Ah, I don't know. I like football better. Where you going?"

"I don't know yet. There don't seem to be a lot of colleges that need a slow catcher."

"You'll pick up someplace. You were fast enough today."

"Barely." I stuck out my hand. "Good luck, Joe. I want to say something to Gary while I've got a chance."

"Sure. We'll see you."

Gary Melcher was sitting on the bench, packing his equipment bag. He glanced up at me and then looked down. I put a hand on his shoulder. "Nice game, Gary. Good playing against you again."

"I should've had it. If I hadn't been standing there flat-footed . . . " His voice caught.

"I don't think so, Gary. It was pretty tall, taller than maybe it looked from your angle. Besides, the real mistake was Jake's when he didn't call for the ball far enough outside. What I did had been done before. He should have known that." He nodded, still not looking up. I gave his shoulder a squeeze. "You take care, huh?"

"You, too, Bull."

A balding, grinning guy in a sport shirt and tie intercepted me as I crossed toward our gang celebrating around Borsheim. "Hi, Mike Cattanach, Arizona State. Hell of a move there, son. Haven't seen that done right in years."

I looked him in the eye. "I want in your program," I said. "I don't need a big scholarship, I just want to play for Arizona State."

His smile wobbled for a second, but then came back on full force. "And we'd love to have you. But we've already got more catchers than we can use. I just don't see you getting much playing time even if you made the team."

"And if you didn't have the other catchers?"

He was catching on. His smiled ruefully. "Son, you're one fine high school catcher. You're a good receiver, you can hit, and you can think. But I had the stopwatch on you, and you're *slow*."

"So, I don't have a prayer of making it in a major college program. Tell me the truth."

"I don't think so, son. I wish I could say otherwise, but . . ." He shrugged.

"And I'm not going to make it to the pros, either."

He sighed. "Look, almost nobody makes it to the pros. I've seen hundreds of high school and college players with fantastic skills, but only a handful were good enough and lucky enough to make it to the majors. It's a great dream to have but never bet the bank on it."

"How about Jeff?"

"Maybe he'll be one of the lucky ones, maybe not. He's a good ballplayer, but he needs some weight, maybe another couple of inches of height, and he's going to have to break a couple of bad habits or he'll never hit a really good curve. Then he'll be a decent college ballplayer. After that . . . " He shrugged. "No one can say."

"I can," I said. "He's gonna make it. You can bank on that." I stuck out my hand. "Thanks for being honest. I've been looking for some straight answers for a year."

"Sure. And, son, you are one gutsy ballplayer. Be proud of that."

I was sitting on the front steps in the last of the light when Jeff came up the walk. "Figured you might come by. Want a Coke?" I asked.

"No, I'm good." He sat down with his back to one of the steps. He sighed. "Jeez, I'm beat. What a day, huh?"

"One to remember. So, did you sign?"

"Yeah, it's done. I start in their summer program in three weeks."

"Full ride?"

"Yeah, my stepdad said it was that or we'd talk to the guy from USC again. Cattanach agreed right off."

"Good. Congratulations."

"Thanks . . . By the way, I brought up your name. Told him he couldn't go wrong signing you."

"What'd he say?"

"Said you'd talked. Too many catchers already in the program."

"And they don't need one who can't break three minutes going to first."

"You're slow, not that slow."

"But too slow."

He didn't answer for a long moment. "Not so slow that you can't play somewhere."

"I don't want to play for some Podunk college. It doesn't mean that much to me anymore. Today was all I needed. Next fall, I'll go down to the U and see if I can rejuvenate some gray cells after all these years of being a jock."

He didn't argue. "So, what are you going to do this summer?"

"In about five minutes, I'm going in and call that girl I know up north. If she'll still see me, I'm going to drive up to McArthur tomorrow."

"Want some company?"

"Not yours. Get your own girl. Take Sally out. She's already got a major-league crush on you, and it'd make her summer."

He laughed. "No, she's a neat kid but way too young. I think Todd Ronchetti's gonna ask her out. He was kind of edging up to her after the game."

"You're missing a chance."

"No, I don't think so. But she is going to make that team a lot of fun. I'm gonna miss that." He gestured toward the street, now almost dark in the minutes before the streetlights came on. "I'm going to miss a lot of this. All the years we played together. All the guys. Billy, especially." He paused, thinking. "You know, it was never quite the same after Billy died."

"No. Not quite."

"Maybe we took it too seriously. It sure felt good to win, but maybe we missed something."

"Well, you always took it too seriously, that's for sure. But you're on your way now."

"Yeah, I guess," he said, and we sat for a long time without speaking, the evening warm about us, as the stars came out and beyond the edge of town, the moon rose on summer.

I drove north the next day to see Bev. She's going to work at Forgotten Pine again this summer, and I'm going to see if I can get my job back, too. But even in the sunshine, with a girl waiting for me and the glow of winning the championship still warming me, I couldn't help but think of other times, other seasons.

No matter what happens in my life from here on in, I think I'll always remember when Jeff and I played catch in the park in sweaters and stocking hats while everybody else in the world stayed inside, out of the autumn wind. I remember how the ball sailed bright through the cold air, the sound of it hitting our gloves sharp and lonely, as the wind blew the last of the fall leaves across the dying grass of the outfield and kicked up eddies of dust on the empty base paths.

Jeff and me, impatient even in November for April and the first pitch of a new season.

ABOUT THIS SCHOLASTIC SIGNATURE AUTHOR

ALDEN R. CARTER'S novels for young people include *Up Country*, an ALA Best of the Best, and *Sheila's Dying*; *Growing Season*; and *Wart, Son of Toad*, which were all selected as ALA Best Books for Young Adults. His Scholastic Press titles are *Between a Rock and A Hard Place* and *Dogwolf*, an *American Bookseller* "Pick of the Lists."

Alden Carter lives in Marshfield, Wisconsin, with his wife, son, and daughter.